"What did you think[...]
Gabe asked.

"Busy, but good. Some things were different than back in Chicago, but a lot was the same, too."

"Like what?"

"The chaos."

He chuckled. "I see. And you don't like the chaos."

"It's fine. I mean, I'm used to it, but my instinct is to control it." Sara shrugged. "Sometimes that isn't always possible."

"No, it's not." He looked at her from under his lashes again. Even out here in the rain forest, her clothes were pristine. Even all those red curls he'd seen the day before that were ready to tumble everywhere were now tamed to within an inch of their life into a neat ponytail at the nape of her neck. Everything about her screamed control freak and yet all Gabe could feel was an unreal urge to muss her up—run his fingers through those curls and free them, see if they felt as soft as they looked, rumple up those clothes of hers while he kissed her silly and…

Dammit. No.

He did flings. Nothing more now. And Sara Parker practically had a neon sign flashing Forever above her head. He should stay away. Far away.

Dear Reader,

After the year that was 2020, I wanted to fly away to a lush tropical paradise and lose myself in a story of hope and healing and happily-ever-afters. And so *Costa Rican Fling with the Doc* was born.

This book contains a "seasoned" romance featuring a fortysomething nurse, Sara Parker, who's raised her son as a single mom and spent over twenty years working as a pediatric intensive care nurse. Now that her son is away at college, she's decided to take early retirement and make some changes in her life, starting with a mission trip to Costa Rica. She's not looking for romance, but the minute she meets Dr. Gabriel Novak, sparks fly!

Fiftysomething Gabe is at a turning point in his life, too. After losing his wife and son during the Croatian War, he's dedicated himself to helping those in need to the exclusion of everything else. As head of Sara's mission trip, he's forced to deal with her and the emotions she stirs inside him— emotions he never expected to feel again.

Can these two let down their walls and allow love into their future?

You'll have to read to find out!

Traci <3

COSTA RICAN FLING WITH THE DOC

TRACI DOUGLASS

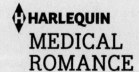

HARLEQUIN
MEDICAL
ROMANCE

HARLEQUIN®
MEDICAL
ROMANCE™

Recycling programs for this product may not exist in your area.

ISBN-13: 978-1-335-40890-7

Costa Rican Fling with the Doc

Harlequin Enterprises ULC
22 Adelaide St. West, 40th Floor
Toronto, Ontario M5H 4E3, Canada
www.Harlequin.com

Printed in U.S.A.

Traci Douglass is a *USA TODAY* bestselling author of contemporary and paranormal romance. Her stories feature sizzling heroes full of dark humor, quick wit and major attitude, and heroines who are smart, tenacious and always give as good as they get. She holds an MFA in Writing Popular Fiction from Seton Hill University, and she loves animals, chocolate, coffee, hot British actors and sarcasm— not necessarily in that order.

Books by Traci Douglass

Harlequin Medical Romance

First Response in Florida

The Vet's Unexpected Hero
Her One-Night Secret

One Night with the Army Doc
Finding Her Forever Family
A Mistletoe Kiss for the Single Dad
A Weekend with Her Fake Fiancé
Their Hot Hawaiian Fling
Neurosurgeon's Christmas to Remember

Visit the Author Profile page at Harlequin.com.

CHAPTER ONE

"WELCOME TO HOSPITAL LOS CABRERAS."

Nurse Sara Parker opened her eyes and found herself sitting alone in an unmoving truck, the glorious air-conditioning long gone. Outside, a cluster of brown and gray buildings surrounded a larger white tent. People were milling about, some dressed in T-shirts, shorts and flip-flops, others in scrubs. She rubbed one cheek then spotted a flash of yellow at the driver side. Legs sticking to the vinyl seat, she yawned, then leaned across the gearshift and cracked open the driver's side window.

"Noah?" Her voice sounded groggy to her own ears as she called to her best friend.

Normally, she wasn't a napper, but after a five-hour flight from Chicago, followed by a two-hour drive on bumpy roads from the Costa Rican capital of San José to this place, she was exhausted.

"Don't think he heard you," another female voice said from the back seat.

Her name was Doreen, and she was a dermatologist from Barrington. Also, at least according to Doreen, a reality TV star on some show called *Doctors of Del Ray*. Sara wouldn't know. She didn't have much time to watch TV these days, what with picking up extra shifts in the PICU back in her home hospital, Chicago Memorial, before leaving on this sabbatical.

If you could call a month in the rain forest volunteering for the charity medical organization her hospital sponsored down here in Central America a sabbatical.

Sara glanced at the other woman in the rearview mirror, then undid her seat belt. Doreen wasn't exactly the type she'd have expected to come down here. From what Sara had read of her pretravel paperwork before arriving, Los Cabreras was far from any urban area and as close to the Nicaraguan border as you could legally get without crossing. Which served its purpose well, since the main function of the field hospital was to treat the many migrants fleeing gang violence and poverty in their own country for the relatively better conditions in Costa Rica.

Still, she doubted Doreen's bleached-blond hair and perfect, camera-ready makeup would last long down here. The woman looked in good enough shape otherwise, though, and from what Sara could see, she was maybe a few years older than Sara's own forty-two. She opened her door. "I'm going to check things out. Want to come?"

"Sure," Doreen said, clambering out behind Sara. "I can't wait to get started."

They started walking around the car, the sweltering air clinging to Sara's skin and pressing down on the back of her neck. Humidity had her auburn curls rioting more than normal, and sweat already prickled her hairline around her forehead. A line of people she assumed were patients jostled nearby, and out of habit, Sara pulled her cell phone from the pocket of her jean shorts, even though the chances of getting a signal way out here were slim to none, and typed in a quick text to her son, Luke.

Arrived at Los Cabreras. Will text more later.

After hitting Send, she glanced through the open flaps of the white tent at what looked like the clinic proper. Near the far end were two exam stations separated by a wall of white canvas. A male doctor worked in each one, assisted by a nurse. It was there she spotted her friend Noah, talking to the doctor on the left. A mix of Spanish and English buzzed around her, the former going far faster than the app she'd used to learn the basics, each missed word or phrase causing the niggle of uncertainty in her gut to bore deeper.

I'm just tired. Things will be better tomorrow. Please let things be better tomorrow.

They'd just peeked inside one of the smaller buildings in the compound at what appeared to be the dental area when Noah called out to them.

"Come on, ladies. Let's grab your bags from the truck and I'll show you where you'll be staying."

He jogged past them, waving at some of the people in line, apparently completely in his element down here. Sara envied him that, considering she'd felt out of sync with her life since her son, Luke, had gone back to college in California a few months ago, leaving her an empty nester again.

Empty being the operative word, since there wasn't much to fill the time when you were a single mother without your kid around.

So yeah, she'd worked a lot, picking up extra shifts to allow her colleagues with families at home to spend more time with them. But there were only so many hours you could work before, eventually, you had to face yourself alone.

At first being on sabbatical had been novel—not getting up at the crack of dawn, not getting called in to work in the middle of the night or on holidays, not having to keep to anyone else's schedule but her own.

That had lasted about a week. Then the boredom had set in, and she'd started think about how she could give back, how she might be able to use her years of experience to help others. News coverage of the gang violence and civil wars down here in Central America had led her to research the charity Noah had left to work for two years prior, and now here she was, seeing a bit of the world and helping people receive desperately needed medical care.

"Here," Noah said to her before handing down her wheeled suitcase from the back of the truck. "What the hell did you pack in there?"

"What?" Sara frowned up at him, squinting against the bright sunshine. "I followed the packing list very carefully."

Noah snorted. "Right. I forgot how anal you are."

"I'm not anal," Sara said, doing her best not to smile, too. "Okay. Maybe I am, but that's what makes me so good at my job."

"Whatever. You're a good nurse because of your heart. You care about people." He snorted. "Even if you are anal."

"Whatever." Sara waited off to the side while Noah got Doreen's bag out, then walked with them to another building across the compound. It was two stories and gray, with bars covering all the exterior windows and the door.

She followed Noah inside and found herself in an office space. Fans whirred in every direction, and towers of paper fluttered in the fake breeze. On the far wall, mismatched picture frames and awards hung in long, perfect lines. It was a far cry from the modern PICU she'd left behind in Chicago, filled with state-of-the-art equipment and modern conveniences.

A bright British accent interrupted her thoughts. "You must be Sara Parker," a blond man, maybe midthirties, said from behind the desk. "I'm Tristan." Noah's partner came around the desk and pulled Sara into an unexpected hug, swaddling her in the scent of soap and a hint of fabric softener. The green of his T-shirt highlighted his blue eyes, and his smile was wide and genuine. Sara liked him immediately. "Great to finally meet you. Noah's told me so much about you."

"All good, I hope," he said, laughing. "And you're as adorable as Noah said, too."

"Excuse me," a tall, dark man said, his accent difficult to place. Eastern European, maybe? Sara glanced up at him and recognized him from inside the tent earlier. He was one of the doctors here.

"Dr. Gabriel Novak," Tristan said, stopping the guy from climbing the stairs. "Let me introduce you to our new arrivals. This is Nurse Sara Parker and Dr. Doreen Dubuque, both from Chicago."

He gave them both a curt nod.

"Nice to meet you," Sara said, extending her hand. "Where are you from?"

"Around," he said, then continued past her. "Sorry, I'm in a bit of a hurry."

"If you're heading upstairs, Gabe," Tristan called after him, "could you take their bags to their room, please?"

He stopped, back to them, his broad shoulders slumping and his aggrieved sigh loud. Sara half expected him to refuse, since most of the doctors she knew from back home wouldn't have deigned to lower themselves to play bellboy. But then, Dr. Gabriel Novak surprised her again by loading himself up like a pack mule with her and Doreen's stuff before hiking up the stairs. Noah was at his heels, leaving them alone with Tristan.

"So, Noah tells me you're on sabbatical for a few months."

She snorted. "Yeah. I tried the rest and relaxation route, but it got old quickly. My son's in college now, and I wanted to see the world before I get too old and feeble, have a few adventures, maybe help some people along the way."

"Well, you've definitely come to the right place. We can use all the help we can get around here."

"That's good then," she said, looking around again.

"And how about you, Dr. Dubuque?" He turned toward Doreen. "Far cry from your posh lifestyle."

"I'm ready for a change," Doreen said, her white smile bright. "Bring it on."

"Oh, we'll bring it, all right." Tristan returned to his seat behind the desk. "Sorry. I'd give you both a tour, but the compound is fairly small, and I need to get this grant request done. We can do that later, after dinner. If either of you are thirsty, there's a cooler of water on the counter there that's safe for drinking and brushing your teeth. You'll be sharing a room upstairs, first one on the left."

"Thanks." Sara smiled, thinking about how fate had brought Noah and Tristan together here in the most unexpected of places. According to her best friend, they'd felt an immediate connection and had been pretty much inseparable ever since. Noah had left his job in pediatric radiology at Chicago Memorial and moved permanently to Costa Rica to be close to his soul mate and help Tristan run the charity operation here. Noah and Sara still kept in regular touch, though, and she'd been thrilled for him, even if it left another empty hole in her life.

She and Doreen climbed the creaking wooden stairs to find their bags in a heap at the top. Sara wheeled hers the short distance into their temporary quarters, then straightened to see an array of photos stuck to the walls, corners curling in the sticky air.

Sara ran her fingers along the edges of each one, taking in the smiling faces. Noah and Tristan. Noah surrounded by a group of children while Dr. Novak stood off to the side.

"Which one do you want?" Doreen asked, pointing to the two twin beds in the room.

"Either's fine." Sara sighed, walking to the small window. On the ground below, a stooped woman carried two chickens by the feet, dangling them upside down, motionless wings splayed wide.

Then she pulled out her cell phone and searched for a signal to connect her to the world.

"That probably won't work this far out of range." Dr. Novak slouched against the door frame, looking far more attractive than any man had a right to in scrubs, all lanky limbs and intense gaze, a shadow of stubble darkening his jaw and his dark hair ruffled. Not that she noticed. Nope. Sara was here to work, not for romance. Besides, handsome men were trouble. She'd learned that lesson the hard way with her ex-husband. "Tristan should've mentioned it, but he forgets when he's busy."

"Oh." Her heart sank a little. She'd talked to Luke before she'd left Chicago, but not since. What if he needed her? He was a grown man now, but cutting those strings was still hard. "Okay. Thanks."

"Do you need to make a call?" he asked.

"I was just going to check in with my son. Let him know I'm all right."

Dr. Novak frowned, and even that look on him was gorgeous. Unfair, really, for one human to be so genetically blessed. "There's a satellite phone downstairs the charity owns for emergencies."

"Well." Sara fidgeted a bit under his gaze, heat rising in her cheeks. "This isn't really an emergency, just a concerned mom thing."

He smiled then, and damn if her breath didn't hitch against her will. "Concerned mothers are always an emergency. Come on. I'm sure Tristan won't mind."

When they got downstairs, though, Tristan was gone. Dr. Novak walked around the desk and riffled through the drawers, finally pulling out the phone. He handed it to her. "You need to dial the country code first."

"Thanks," Sara said, but he was already halfway out the front door.

She dialed her son's number then waited for the call to connect. One ring. Two.

"Luke."

"Hey, it's Mom."

"Hey! Are you there yet?" he asked.

She turned toward the wall, and her eyes filled with unexpected tears. It wasn't like her to cry, but it was just so good to hear his voice. "Yes. We finally got to the field hospital about an hour ago." Sara put her back against the wall and slid down to the floor with the phone pressed to her ear. "I'm starting to think maybe this wasn't a very good idea. Maybe I should come home. What if something happens?"

"What's going to happen?" Luke asked. "You'll be fine. I'll be fine. Everyone's fine, Mom."

A beat passed.

"Seriously. I thought we talked about this. You put your life on hold for me growing up. Now it's your turn to pursue your dreams." His voice was a mash of sternness and warmth beyond his years. How times had changed. Seemed like just yesterday she'd been the one to talk him through difficult times. Like when his bike had been stolen in elementary school. Or his beloved pet guinea pig died. Or his appendix had ruptured junior year of high school. Now the tables were turned, and Sara felt off kilter.

"Tell me the truth," she said. "Are you doing

all right with your classes? Not partying too much? Being careful? Using condoms?"

"God. Mom." He gave an exasperated huff, and she smiled despite herself. "Yes. Stop embarrassing me. What about you? Any hot doc volunteers?"

For some reason her mind flashed an image of Dr. Novak, but she quickly brushed it aside.

Static cut through their connection.

"Mom? You still there?"

"I'm here." She exhaled slow.

"I need to go. Have fun. Enjoy the trip. Meet new people. You'll be great."

Luke was probably right. She just wasn't very good at doing things for herself. Sara shrugged. "Okay."

"Oh, and Mom?" Luke said. "I'm proud of you. You'll be glad you did this. I promise."

CHAPTER TWO

GABE FINISHED UP with his last patient in the clinic around dusk. It was a little girl named Chuly whose mother had been diagnosed with dengue fever. They'd walked for two days through the rain forest where they'd been hiding to get to the hospital, and little Chuly had fallen and broken her arm along the way. They'd put a temporary splint on it when she'd arrived, but the main priority at that time was the mother, who'd been hemorrhaging from her nose and mouth and had passed out in the clinic.

He'd tested her platelet count and found it abnormally low. Gabe had intubated the woman and currently had her sedated and on a ventilator while they got her hydrated with an IV and got her temperature under control.

"I want my mommy," Chuly cried in Spanish, her little face red. "Please!"

His heart pinched tight, and Gabe turned away, fiddling with the casting kit to hide his expression. He'd thought it would get easier over the years, hiding his pain, but it didn't. Especially at times like this.

"Want me to find a bed for her tonight, Doc?" Noah asked.

"Yes," Gabe said. "Near her mother, please."

"But—" Noah started, frowning.

"No." Gabe looked at him then. "Children need to see what's happening, need to know. I'll take her. You get the bed ready."

"Sure, Doc." Noah left, his tone dubious.

Gabe knew the others saw his ways as unorthodox sometimes, but he understood better than most what trauma did to a person if it was buried or ignored. He finished disposing of the used kit, then putting the girl's arm in a sling before crouching before her and smiling.

"I'll take you to see your mommy now," Gabe said in Spanish. "Ready?"

Chuly nodded and held out her free arm for Gabe to pick her up.

He did, then walked to the other end of the tent and behind a curtained-off area. "Here's your mommy. She's sleeping right now, because we're giving her medicine to feel better. She can't talk to you, either, because we have a tube helping her breathe. But she can hear you and knows that you're there. And soon, she'll wake up again and be so glad to see you. Noah's making up a bed for you, and you can sleep near her tonight, okay? No need to be afraid of her or the machines, all right?"

Chuly blinked at her mother, then at the monitors surrounding her, then at Gabe. Finally, she nodded, fingers stuck in her mouth. *"Gracias."*

"You're welcome." He kissed her temple, then settled her on the bed before tucking her in. "If you need anything at all, just call. There's someone right on the other side of that curtain all night to help."

The little girl turned on her side to face her mother, fingers still in her mouth, though she'd calmed considerably. Gabe slowly withdrew, not wanting to startle the child, then finally left the tent, tired and restless and hungry.

His stomach growled, and a glance at his watch showed he'd missed dinner with the others. Guess he'd walk into the little village down the road to eat. First, though, he needed to change clothes.

He went upstairs and took a quick shower, then put on fresh shorts and a T-shirt before heading out again. Nearly made it, too, except for the soft sound of snoring coming from the last room on the left.

Normally, Gabe kept to himself on these trips. He'd been on more volunteer medical crews than he could count the past twenty or so years, worked with hundreds of people, treated even more, but for some reason, he couldn't seem to get Sara Parker out of his mind.

The door stood open, and Gabe peeked inside to find her sprawled across the bed, on top of the covers, mouth open and snoring softly. "Hello?"

No answer.

He tried again, a little louder this time, stepping into the room. "Sara? Are you awake?"

She shot up, blinking and rubbing her eyes, her red hair going everywhere. "I'm awake. I'm awake." Sara looked around the room, as if trying to figure out where she was.

"You're in Costa Rica. At Los Cabreras," he said. "Looks like you've been asleep for a while."

"What time is it?" An errant curl fell across her forehead, and her pink T-shirt scrunched up, revealing a small swath of creamy skin. Gabe knew he should look away but couldn't.

"Around 7:00 p.m. Did you have dinner with the others?"

She frowned; her nose scrunched. "No. I must've missed it. I'll be okay. I have some granola bars."

"No, she won't." Noah's voice drifted in from down the hallway. "If you're going to Alma's, take her with you. She needs real food."

Gabe rubbed his temple, then gestured toward the stairs. "You might as well come. There's no arguing with him."

Twenty minutes later, they walked along the red dirt road into the village. Thin, fingerlike leaves of mango trees stirred around them, tossed by the wind wafting in from the distant ocean. Things were quiet at this time of day, but come morning the road would be busy again.

Within a few minutes, they arrived at a small restaurant. Gabe took a deep breath and pulled out Sara's chair, hoping the smells of garlic and searing-hot cooking oil seeping from every corner of the narrow dining room would relax him. They always had in the past.

He been coming here since his very first mission trip with the charity two decades prior, still acclimating to life outside Croatia, still mourning the loss of his family back home. Even then, the owner of the place, an older woman named Alma, always found an extra bottle of Imperial beer, placing it in front of him in exchange for a smile. After the first year or two, his smiles came without prompting.

Gabe stared at the poster on the wall above Sara's head for Costa Rica's soccer team La Sele while she sat across the table, staring at the tattered paper menu with the same three options they always had.

"Need help choosing?" he asked.

"No, I can read Spanish better than I speak it." Pink crept up her cheeks, and she finally met his gaze. "Thanks, though."

"Sure." Gabe exhaled slow, his gaze flicking between his own menu and the bow of Sara's lips. *Whoops. Nope.* He cleared his throat and scowled at his own menu. "No problem."

She nodded.

Silence.

"What's this?" Sara pointed to a line on the menu.

"You don't want that."

She gave him a flat look. "But what is it?"

"Guinea pig."

Sara blinked. "Guinea pig?"

"Yep."

She laughed. "Yeah, you're right. I don't want that."

Eager to distract himself from the unwanted awareness tingling through him, Gabe asked, "Where did you learn Spanish?"

"High school. But that was thirty years ago, and I've forgotten more than I learned."

"I guarantee by the end of the trip, you'll understand more."

Alma came to take their orders then, her wide smile crinkling her weathered face. Gabe hugged her.

"Who's the pretty American?" she whispered near his ear.

Gabe shook his head. That's why he never brought volunteers here. Too many questions. "Nurse. She's part of the new mission trip," he said, then kissed Alma on both cheeks, ignoring the questions in the woman's eyes.

"I'll have the enchiladas, *por favor*."

They both turned to Sara, and she attempted to order, rubbing her forehead between words. It wasn't perfect, but she managed to ask for the chicken soup.

"Good choice," Gabe said as Alma shuffled back into the kitchen.

Sara covered her face with her hands. "I can't believe how horrible I sounded."

"Hey, you're trying." Without thinking, he reached across the table and pried her hands away, his voice softening as his fingers tangled with hers. "That's all anyone can ask."

Their eyes locked a moment, and Gabe swallowed hard, then quickly let her go. He needed to move, so he stood and sidled behind the nearby counter, desperate for something to ease the sudden energy zinging through him. Gabe grabbed two beers from the refrigerator then called down the hall to the kitchen, "*Dos Imperials.*"

Sara watched him, wide-eyed, as he returned to the table. "Is that okay? To just take them like that? I mean, I don't want to end up in Costa Rican jail."

Gabe watched her over the rim of his bottle. "You've been in Costa Rican jail?"

"No." She blushed prettily. "But my son goes to college in California, and you hear things."

"Ah." He nodded. "He has been in Costa Rican jail."

"What? No!" Her cheeks flamed hotter, and from where Gabe sat, it was hard to tell where her auburn hair ended and her face began. "Luke would never… I mean, I heard about it on TV."

"I'm joking, Sara." He pushed her beer closer to her tightly laced fingers and laughed, letting her off the hook at last. "We won't go to jail. Alma's a friend of mine."

"Oh." She flashed him a tentative smile. "Could I maybe have a soda instead, then? Not sure I can handle alcohol right now."

"Sure." He returned her bottle of Imperial to the fridge, then grabbed her a soda instead.

"Thank you, Dr. Novak," she said when he returned and placed the can in front of her. "What's your specialty?"

"Emergency medicine," he answered. "And please, call me Gabe."

"Do you like it, Gabe?"

He had, in the beginning. The adrenaline rush, the life-or-death situations. Then a bomb had fallen on his family's apartment building in Vukovar, and everything had changed. Now medicine was just something he did to help others, his penance for his failures. There wasn't enough beer in the world to numb that kind of pain. Which was why he didn't talk about it. To anyone. Especially sexy nurses he'd just met. So, instead, he just shrugged. "It has its moments." He took another long swallow of beer as their food arrived. "How do you feel about monkeys?"

"Monkeys?" Sara's spoon halted halfway to her mouth, golden broth dribbling from the edges. "Uh, I don't know. I've never met one."

He held up a finger for her to wait, then jogged down the hall, returning moments later with a small guest on a leash. The spider monkey sat in the chair between them, his face turned toward Sara.

Wide-eyed, she looked between him and the monkey. "What's his name? Is he friendly?"

"Don Juan, and yes. He's very friendly. Probably too friendly." Gabe held out a finger, and the little monkey grabbed on, like a handshake. Sara's smile made Gabe's pulse stumble despite his wishes.

"Can I try?" she asked, and he nodded, not trusting his voice just then.

She held out her index finger, and the monkey shook it, then stole a carrot from her bowl.

Broth splashed everywhere, leaving a slosh of yellow across her shirt. Sara laughed then pulled the last vegetables from her bowl for Don Juan, who gobbled them down, then climbed into her lap, as if he owned her.

Lucky monkey.

Gabe scowled, shoving that unsettling thought aside.

What the hell is wrong with me?

That was a long list in his mind, but nothing explained why he felt such an immediate, unwanted attraction to a woman he'd just met. He didn't do romance or relationships or close ties of any kind, really. Not since losing Marija and his two-year-old son, Karlo.

"Where did he come from?" Sara asked, jarring him from his thoughts.

"I found him last year when I was here. Some kids had found him in the rain forest and were tormenting him."

"Aw. That's awful." Sara cooed, stroking the tiny monkey's head, "Did they hurt you?"

"His leg was broken. Probably how the kids caught him so easily. I set it at the clinic." Gabe shrugged. "But please don't tell Tristan. He'll be pissed if he finds out I used supplies on a monkey."

Sara looked up from the monkey and winked, sending Gabe's traitorous heart stumbling like a drunken sailor. "Our secret."

Once their meal was over, they left Alma's and headed back toward the clinic.

Twilight gathered as they walked back toward the compound, a chorus of cicadas swelling around them. Muffled voices drifted from the barred windows of the homes lining the street, and Gabe couldn't help stealing glances at the woman beside him as they fell into step together.

"Thanks for dinner," Sara said.

"No problem."

One house away from the compound gates, a man shuffled along, talking to himself, a near-empty liquor bottle in one hand. Gabe's protective instincts went on high alert, and without thinking, he yanked Sara closer into his side, wrapping an arm around her shoulders as the drunk stumbled past them.

Most likely the man wasn't a threat to anyone except himself, but Gabe didn't take chances.

Not anymore.

Not outside the trauma room, anyway.

In the breeze, he caught a hint of her shampoo as her curls brushed his jaw. His chest squeezed tight, and he almost inhaled deeper, but then he let Sara go fast instead.

"What was that all about?" she asked, rubbing her arms as she stumbled slightly on her flip-flops.

Ignoring her question, he unlatched the metal gate to the compound and motioned her through. "Nothing. Just being careful. And you should change shampoo. That sweet, fruity-smelling stuff will draw bugs around here."

Not romantic at all. But then, that was the point.

As she stood staring at him in the darkness, Gabe turned away and headed for the main house. The other new arrival, the silly woman with the makeup and hair, hurried past him toward Sara. While Gabe continued on alone, he could hear the woman's voice behind him talking to Sara.

"I'm glad you're back. I could use someone to talk to about the email I got for the next season of *Doctors of Del Ray...*"

CHAPTER THREE

THE NEXT MORNING, Sara got her first good look around the compound before clinic started for the day. Spiked *pochote* trees bent enough for her to make out the shapes of the surrounding houses outside the tall chain-link fencing that formed the perimeter of their area, the sun reflecting off the homes' metal roofs. Inside the compound, a line had already formed, and at least thirty people waited for treatment, from what she could see. All ages and conditions.

"*Hola,*" Gabe said as he passed Sara on his way into the white clinic tent.

He was dressed in blue scrubs this morning and looking far too perky and perfect for so early in the day. At six four, he stood a good foot taller than most of the villagers. They waved and grinned at him like he was a dear friend.

"Pretty good turnout, huh?" Noah asked, coming up to stand beside Sara.

"Looks like it," Sara said. "What should I do today?"

"Assist Gabe with cases. That should give you a feel for what it's like here. Once you're comfortable, then we'll assign you a specific duty." He smiled at her over his shoulder. "But first, let me give you a tour of the compound, since you were too busy sleeping and eating with Gabe last night to see it then."

She gave her friend a look, then laughed. "Whatever. I had jet lag. Sue me."

"Nice try. Costa Rica's central time, same as Chicago. Only difference here is we stay the same year-round instead of losing an hour in the spring. You were just tired and cranky, and you know it." Noah laughed. "Don't think I've forgotten those early-morning shifts at the hospital with you already."

Sara shook her head and followed him toward the entrance gate. "Fine. I was exhausted. For some reason airports always do that to me. I take exception to the cranky part, though. Give me my caffeine and no one gets hurt."

"I'll make sure the pot's always brewing first thing in the morning for you, then."

Noah stood with her at the front of the compound and began pointing out locations. "Okay. So, you already know the offices, dorms and kitchens. And in the center here is the main clinic/general hospital tent. Behind that is the surgical tent. We have the capacity to do up to twenty surgeries a day, if needed." He pointed to another area to the right. "The gray building there is our ICU, then the four smaller white tents across the road there are the twenty-bed unit ward. Behind them is our latrine and our shower facilities." They turned and looked left next. "And over there are the lab, X-ray, supply storage and dispensary."

"Wow. Looks like you guys have everything you need out here," Sara said, gazing around at everything. "Seems bigger today than it did last night. How many patients do you typically treat a day here?"

"Anywhere from fifty to a hundred, depending on the season and our staffing. It's taken us a couple of years to build it all up, but Tristan's done an amazing job getting grants for the charity, and Gabe has done his part, too. Since he came to work with us two years ago, our turnout had doubled. The patients really connect with him, and he seems to understand their plight. And yeah, we need to have everything we need here, since the closest city hospital is almost two hours away."

"Yikes."

They continued on toward the main clinic/ general hospital tent.

"Where's he from?" Sara asked, curious since she'd gotten precious little info out of the doc last night. "Gabe, I mean. I can't seem to place his accent."

"Croatia," Noah said, stopping outside the tent entrance and glancing at the growing line of people. "Had a pretty rough time of it there, too, back in the '90s, from what I can piece together. Guy doesn't like to talk about himself much."

"Oh, good," Sara said, then chuckled at Noah's side-eye. "I just mean, I thought it was me he didn't like last night, but you make it sound like he's like that with everyone."

"Like what?" Gabe asked from his exam area at the back of the tent.

Man, he must have bat-like hearing. Sara made a mental note to be careful around the guy.

Well, more careful, considering her strange, unwanted awareness of him.

"Nothing," Noah called back to him then shook his head. "We'll open up soon. I just need to get an initial head count for Tristan first. Helps him with his grant applications. You good here?"

"Yep." Sara smiled up at her friend. Same messy light brown hair, same sparkling brown eyes she remembered fondly from the PICU. "I'll get familiar with where everything's at in here before we start."

"Sounds good."

He went back outside, and she walked through the tent, making note of the registration desk up front, the lines of tables and chairs on either side of the tent, where she assumed the nurses took vitals and medical histories and gave vaccine shots, then moved next to the exam area. Four rooms, each separated by white divider walls, complete with beds, equipment and supplies. In the second one on the right stood Gabe.

"Ready for today?" he asked, hanging a stethoscope around his neck.

"I think so. I've worked in pediatric intensive care for eighteen years, plus did rotations in ER during nursing school, so there's not much I haven't seen."

"Remember that later," he said, winking as he walked past her toward the entrance.

Her heart did a weird little somersault in her chest. Not caused by nerves, but from that odd tingling sensation that filled her insides whenever the man was around. She didn't like it. Not one bit. The last thing she needed right now was to get involved with someone like Gabe, no matter how attractive. Since her divorce ten years ago, she'd had flings, sure, but nothing serious. And she liked it that way.

Liked the freedom. Liked not having messy strings attached. Strings meant heartache.

From all the vibes Mr. Tall, Dark and Brooding there gave off, he was nothing but a mess of entanglements.

A needle-thin man with a patchy black beard came in dressed in worn green scrubs and took a seat at the front desk. She'd not met him before but assumed he'd be acting as their registrar for the day.

"Hey, Julio," Gabe said, walking back in and nodding toward the new arrival. They chatted in Spanish for a moment before Gabe headed toward Sara again, a large white bag in his hands. He dropped it at her feet, then smiled. "Do you know how to ask someone's age in Spanish?"

"Yes."

"Good." He pointed toward the bag. "In between assisting me with exams, go around to every child in the tent and ask them their age. If they're under eighteen, give them one of these mosquito nets to take home with them."

"Okay." She picked up one, running her fingers over the fine baby-blue nylon netting. "What about the adults?"

"We don't have enough for them right now. We'll get them later."

Sara nodded. "Right. I'm on it."

The next hour or so rushed by in a whirl of patients and vitals checks and triage of more serious patients. Once she got into the flow of things, it wasn't much different than being back in Chicago—well, except for the whole language barrier thing. But she did the best she could, and the patients were, well, patient enough with her.

She finished up yet another vaccination on an infant and sent the mother and baby on their way, then turned to the next person in line. She'd also handed out most of her bag of mosquito nets already.

"Hola. Por qué estas aquí hoy?" She smiled at the older man, then noticed his pinkie finger

dangling at an odd angle. Guess that answered the question of why he'd come to clinic.

In broken English the man explained he'd hurt his hand on his farm and hiked two days to get to the hospital.

"Oh, goodness." Sara got up and walked him over to Gabe's exam area. "This poor gentleman needs a splint, I think."

Gabe glanced over from the patient he was working with. "Let him sit over there." He hiked his chin toward a row of nearby chairs along the side of the tent. "I'll be with him shortly. And if you could come back here a second when you're done, Sara?"

"Sure." She got the man situated then returned to the exam area. "What's up?"

"I'd like a witness, just in case this turns out to be something more," he said.

"Something more?" Sara looked from him to a girl of about fifteen, who waited in silence on the exam table, staring down at her sandaled feet and biting her lip. Ah. Right. Back in her ER rotation she'd worked several assault cases and knew how delicate they could be. "Whatever you need."

"Good." Gabe looked back at the patient. "She thinks she's pregnant."

The girl looked up then, her eyes glassy

with fear, and spoke in a rapid-fire mix of Spanish and the indigenous Huetar and Rama of the area. Far too fast for Sara to pick up.

"Why do you think you're pregnant?" Gabe asked in Spanish, his expression carefully blank.

The girl bit her lips and shook her head. Sara wasn't sure if the girl was afraid to tell them or if, given how young she was, she might not know. Gabe gave Sara a look, and she reached past him for a urine cup from the supply bin, then stepped closer to the girl, smiling as she introduced herself in Spanish.

"Hi, I'm Sara. I'm a nurse. If you come with me, I'll take you to the bathroom for a sample."

It took a moment, but the girl finally slid down off the exam table and followed Sara out of the tent and back to the latrine area. While the patient got her sample, Sara walked back to the exam area, where Gabe waited.

"Do you think it was part of the gang violence?" she asked, keeping an eye out for the girl to return.

"Not sure." Gabe scowled down at the chart. "But I wouldn't be surprised. I've seen it before."

Sara took that in. She wanted to ask him

more about that, but before she could, the girl came back in with the full urine cup.

"Okay. Let me test this quickly." She put on gloves and took the cup, then dipped a rapid pregnancy test into it. A tense minute passed as they waited for the results, the controlled chaos of the clinic adding to the stress.

Finally, the results came up.

Negative.

The girl visibly relaxed and grinned for the first time since arriving in the tent.

Gabe muttered something under his breath that Sara didn't catch, then reached into a drawer and pulled out a sleeve of condoms and handed them to the girl. "If you and your boyfriend are going to screw around, be responsible."

"*Gracias.*" The girl stuffed them in the pocket of her dress before darting off with a muffled thanks.

"Well, then." Sara stepped over to clean the exam table for the next patient. "You must've been some interesting places on these mission trips."

"Why do you say that?" Gabe asked, washing his hands and not looking at her.

"You said earlier you'd seen gang violence and rapes. That can't have been easy to—"

"It wasn't on a mission trip." He yanked paper towels out of the dispenser with more force than necessary and walked out of the exam area toward the man with the broken finger, leaving Sara behind to stare after him.

She'd obviously said the wrong thing somewhere but wasn't sure exactly what or when.

He took the man to the X-ray area, and Sara went back to her table, far more intrigued by the enigmatic doc than she wanted to be. She was here to work, to see the world. That was it. She had no business becoming interested in a man that...

"Nurse Parker?" Gabe called to her from the back of the tent. "I could use some help."

Sara was on her feet and headed to the exam area again in a flash.

Working closely, they got the man's finger set and splinted and gave him medication for the pain.

It felt good to be needed again. And the fact she felt Gabe's warmth through his scrubs, saw his concern for his patients in his eyes and heard his appreciation for her efforts in his tone had nothing to do with it.

Nope. Not at all.

After they got through the line of patients in the early afternoon, Gabe told everyone on their team to pack up their supply bags and they'd hike out to a nearby smaller village to do some house calls and rechecks of patients who hadn't made it into the clinic that day.

Sara was fine with that, eager to explore more of this area. She quickly refilled her supply bag, then followed Noah and the other medics out of the tent and out of the compound. Gabe led them up a winding, narrow path in a nearby cliff face obscured by spindly branches and lush leaves growing between the cracks. Her shoulders soon ached with the weight of her pack, the strap rubbing and chafing her sensitive skin, and she didn't dare look down. Heights didn't usually bother her, but then, she wasn't usually walking next to a thousand-foot drop, either. Okay, fine. Maybe it wasn't quite that tall, but it certainly felt like it at the moment. As they ascended, Gabe rhythmically chopped through the brush blocking their path with a machete, leaving a trail of severed branches behind him.

Once they reached the top, Sara looked around the flat field that comprised the summit. From up here, the Rio Frio river below looked like a tiny trickling creek and the compound like an elaborate child's play set. Waist-high grasses slapped her legs as they continued onward, and only a single twisted, gnarled tree grew out of the earth, its branches long dead and full of decay. Tree stumps dotted the landscape as well, partially hidden in the swaying grass, growing closer and closer together the longer they walked.

"What happened up here?" she asked, frowning.

"Logging," Noah said from beside her, her face reflected in his mirrored shades.

They kept walking, and soon the field gave way to hard-beaten earth and a trio of small, giggly girls blocking their path. Their thin cotton dresses were covered in patterns of apples, cherries and unicorns. The girls fell silent as they looked past Gabe to Sara. They blinked at her, again and again.

"*Hola*," Gabe said, waving to them.

"*Hola*," the tallest girl replied, her gaze never leaving Sara.

She smiled and waved. "*Hola. Me llamo Sara.*"

The two smaller girls ducked behind their leader, who sized her up then backed away, crying, "*Su pelo! Es rojo como una bruja! Una bruja!*"

The other two girls shrieked, then all three

darted off, footsteps pounding the dry ground, dust flying behind them. The tall one, Sara noticed, listed to the right as she ran, falling behind her friends.

"What did she say?" Sara asked Noah, frowning.

"She's surprised you have red hair. They've probably never seen it before." Noah hooked arms with her as they moved forward.

Finally, they reached a cluster of houses. Between the homes, people stared in their direction while cows meandered through fenced-in pastures behind them.

Suddenly self-conscious about her hair, Sara patted her ponytail and hurried behind the rest of the group into the nearest home. Her eyes slowly adjusted from the brightness outside, and she glanced around the space. Neat, tidy, if a bit stifling with the heat. Even with the windows open and the fans going, it had to be at least ninety in here.

A stout woman stood before them, her black hair cut short, highlighting her wide smile as she hugged Sara first, then Noah. Noah launched into a string of rapid-fire Spanish as he kissed the woman's cheek, pointing at Sara. The woman nodded, then led them through the house to a back patio area, where the air was thankfully cooler. A large table was set up for a meal there, and Gabe had already taken a seat at the far end and now appeared to be in deep in conversation with the taller girl from the summit. Sara caught the girl sneaking glances her way past Gabe.

She turned to Noah. "I thought we were doing house calls and rechecks."

"We are." Noah grinned. "Sometimes that includes more than medical care here." He hiked his chin toward Gabe at the end of the table. "Like Luciana there. She's Doña Lynda's eldest daughter. Last time we were here, she had dengue fever. Her temp was so high, Gabe thought she might die. She couldn't walk. We stayed here at their house for two extra days until she was better."

"Wow." Sara continued to watch Gabe and the girl. He smiled, his dimple on full display while the child talked animatedly, her hands waving in every direction. She reminded Sara of Luke when he'd been younger.

"Come on," Noah said, nodding toward the table. "Make yourself comfortable. The food's excellent here."

Soon, the patio bristled with energy, and Sara forgot all about the heat as Doña Lynda moved between the house and the yard, bringing in plate after plate of yumminess. Everything from tamales and tacos to *olla de carne*—a savory mix of cassava, carrots, corn, plantains, taro root and other local vegetables. And for dessert, *tres leches* cake and *arroz con leche*, a mixture of rice and milk flavored with sugar, salt, lemon zest and cinnamon sticks.

Doreen sat next to the team's dentist, Matteo, eating and playing a game of peekaboo with a toddler while chattering on about the next season of her reality show.

"I thought that show got canceled," Noah said, frowning.

"No. We're just on hiatus for now," Doreen said, looking away fast.

While they ate, Luciana stood in the doorway, then shuffled forward until she stood within arm's reach of Sara. This close, Sara could see the tufts of baby hair escaping her ponytail, but she didn't give any indication of it, not wanting to startle the poor girl again. Luciana wound her arms tightly behind her back and shifted from one sandaled foot to the other.

Finally, the girl reached into the pocket of

her unicorn dress and held out a single green orb to Sara.

Careful not to touch fingers, she took it. "*Gracias.*"

Luciana backed away again, stumbling over people's feet until she huddled next to Gabe once more. He put down his fork and whispered something in her ear. Next thing Sara knew, the girl ran back to her, stopping a foot away.

"*De nada,*" Luciana said in a rush, then tore out of the house.

"What is it?" Sara asked once the girl had left, holding up her gift. A few rough brown lines cut through the tough green skin.

"It's a coconut." Gabe waggled his fingers for Sara to give it to him. He pulled out a small pocketknife and cut an oblong hole in the top of it before handing it back to her. "Drink the water. It's good, I promise."

She did, bringing the fruit to her lips and tipping her head back, taking a small sip. It was sweet and tangy at the same time. Good, just like Gabe said. She took another swallow, then another, until she'd drained it dry. She caught Gabe's eye and felt a weird flutter inside. Okay. Maybe the man wasn't completely horrible. Kids seemed to like him just fine. And he did seem to know about good food. Take today and last night at Alma's, for example.

"It's good, yes?" he asked from the end of the table.

"Yes. It's good. Thanks." Sara forced her gaze away from his, staring at the empty fruit in her hand instead.

After dinner, some of their team split off to take a walk around the other houses up here, while Sara, Noah and Gabe stayed on the patio with Mrs. Lynda. Noah and their hostess were soon in a heated discussion over some book they'd both read. As they talked, Sara became aware that Luciana was back, this time taking a seat close by Sara, her calves peeking out from beneath the hem off her dress as she swung her feet off the floor.

A distinct smell of antiseptic came from the girl. The same antiseptic they used in the clinic.

Apparently, Sara wasn't the only one who noticed it, either, because next thing she knew Gabe was there, looking decidedly unhappy.

"Luciana?" he said, holding up a ruined pack of wipes. "*Qué es esto?*"

The girl stared down at her toes and shrugged.

"What happened?" Sara asked, frowning.

"It appears Luciana was curious about what was in our medical packs."

"Oh." Sara snatched the now-empty package from him and crumpled it up. "No harm done. We've got more back at the compound."

He sat down on the other side of her, still scowling. "I don't like to waste supplies. You never know when you might run out."

"It's fine." She stuffed the empty pack in her pocket. "You've obviously never raised a child before. Their philosophy is what's yours is mine and what's mine is mine."

She chuckled, then stopped when Gabe didn't laugh with her. And yes, it had been a pretty lame joke, but that didn't explain the desolate look on his face. She wanted to ask more, but he focused on Luciana instead. Sara glanced over, too, and spotted a flash of purple sticking out from the front pocket of her dress.

"What have you got there?" Gabe pointed. The girl lowered her eyes and pulled out an index card, also from the clinic. He handed it to Sara. "Here."

She took not sure what to do now. She got being thrifty with your things, but it was just one card. Sara pulled out a pen instead. "How do I ask if she wants to play tic-tac-toe?"

He asked the girl for her.

Luciana nodded, eyes wide. Sara handed her the pen to go first. As the played, Gabe got up and walked around to the girl's other side and began examining her damaged leg.

"Do you have kids?" Luciana asked Sara in Spanish.

"I do. A son named Luke. He's twenty-one this year."

"Wow." Luciana made a line through the game she'd won and started another for them. "Where do you live?"

"Chicago." At the girl's blank look, Sara added, "It's a city in the US."

"Does it snow there?"

"Yes, lots sometimes."

She asked Luciana if she'd like to see a picture of the snow, and the girl nodded. Sara reached into the pocket of her medical pack, where she'd stashed her wallet with her ID. Inside, she pulled out a picture from a few years back, taken at a fund-raiser for the hospital back in Chicago. The party had been formal, and for once she'd dressed up, wearing her favorite little black dress with a deep V in the front. She didn't realize until too late that Gabe was staring at it along with Luciana.

"Wow." His voice sounded rougher and deeper than usual, which sent off an odd tingling in Sara's gut. "You look...wow."

"Thanks." Heat prickled her cheeks. "This was taken a while ago at a party at the hospital where I work."

"Princess?" Luciana asked in English. The girl was practically in Sara's lap now, all reticence gone.

"No." Sara laughed and shook her head.

Luke had been with her that night as her date. He'd looked so grown-up and sophisticated in his tailored suit that had matched Sara's dress. In the photo, he stood with his arm looped around her waist, a broad smile on his face.

Unlike Gabe's brooding scowl as he turned back to focus on Luciana's leg. So much for their nice moment.

As they continued their game, with Sara losing again, Gabe examined the little girl's atrophied calf muscle, then checked her muscle strength.

"Everything okay?" Sara asked him under her breath.

"Luciana contracted dengue fever from a mosquito bite the last time we were here, and she had a high fever for many days and couldn't walk."

"That's what Noah said. But she's doing better now, right?"

"Yes, but this leg is still weak." He held them side by side to demonstrate the difference in muscle mass for Sara. "See?"

Sara nodded, and Gabe made a series of funny faces to keep Luciana happy long enough for him to finish his exam. When he was done, he patted the girl on the head, then sent her outside, the smell of antiseptic wafting behind her.

"So, what's your prognosis, Doctor?" Sara asked once Luciana was gone.

"Not sure." He took a deep breath, looking a bit defeated. "There's no way to do a full assessment out here. I'd need to see her at the compound." Gabe brushed off his scrub pants and headed for the door, then turned back to Sara, his remote expression firmly back in place. "We open the clinic at noon tomorrow. We'll start back down soon, so everyone can get their rest."

Sara figured they'd hike down the same way they came up after stopping into the rest of the houses to say hello and check on the residents. Instead, they hiked to the other end of the small village, where the five of them sat, then stood, then sat some more. Noah dug a book out of his bag and leaned against Doreen, devouring the pages. Sara had forgotten how much he loved to read. When they took breaks together at the hospital, he constantly had his nose stuffed between the pages of a story, ignoring everyone else in the cafeteria.

"What are we doing here, exactly?" she asked Gabe.

"Waiting on our ride back to the compound."

"Oh." She turned to look into the distance, squinting her eyes in the setting sun. This side of the hill was less steep, and through the tall grass, she could see a road winding. A cool breeze blew and gnats swarmed and Sara let herself relax.

"You look deep in thought," Gabe said, taking a seat on the ground beside her, resting his elbows atop his knees, the soft cotton of his blue scrubs hinting intriguingly at the body beneath. The man was an enigma wrapped in a mystery—hot one minute, cold toward her the next, and she doubted she'd ever figure him out. Not that she was going to try. Nope.

Sara stared at her hands.

"Listen, I came across as a bit abrupt earlier and I'm sorry…" he started.

"It's okay," she said. "You don't really know me."

"No. I don't." He shook his head. "But that isn't an excuse to be rude."

She took that in a moment, let it settle. He was making an attempt, at least. "I appreciate the apology."

"You're welcome." He flashed her a brief grin, full of adorable dimple, and those damned flutters started up in her gut again, without her consent.

Quickly, she switched subjects at a distraction. "So, tell me what you do when you're not at Los Cabreras." She squinted over at him, shielding her eyes with her hand. "Do you work in a regular hospital down here as well?"

He shrugged. "I sometimes fill in at the medical center in San José, when they need me. Noah and Tristan, too. The same charity that funds Los Cabreras is affiliated with them, too."

"What about Matteo?" They both looked over to where he was stretched out on the other side of Doreen, eyes closed, their hands touching. "He's a dentist, right?"

"Yep. He's got his own practice in San José."

A low rumble started in the distance and Sara looked over, expecting a vehicle on the road, but there was none.

"Thunder," Gabe said.

"Oh." She looked up at the sky. It was blue as ever, no clouds. "Do you think it's going to rain?"

"Maybe." He shrugged, his shoulder brushing hers and sending prickles of awareness down her arm.

Okay. Enough.

Sara took a deep breath. This was not what she was here for. Romance was not on her cards. She just wanted to live a little, experience life, see some of the world and help people along the way. So why the hell, out here in the middle of the rain forest, did she have to run into the first man she'd been way more than attracted to in years? And yes, she'd had her share of dates and one-nighters since her divorce a decade prior, but honestly, maybe she hadn't really slowed down enough to recognize it since Luke was born. Now that she was here, Gabe seemed to be everywhere. His arm bumped hers again, as if in confirmation. She sighed and kicked a stone with the toe of her shoe, trying to be polite instead of running as far and as fast as she could, like her common sense warned her to do. "Tell me more about you."

"Like what?" Gabe scowled at the horizon, then her.

Enigma. Mystery. Yep.

"Like, I don't know. What do you do for fun when you aren't working?"

"Not much. I go into the village sometimes." He grinned again, dimple and all, and it was like the stupid sun rose again. *Ugh.* "Go to the bar. Visit friends."

"Huh."

He rolled onto his back, all lithe muscle and tantalizing sinew. She did her best not to look and failed.

What the hell is wrong with me?

"What about you?"

She gave up and stretched out beside him, the grass tickling the back of her neck around her ponytail. "I watch TV. Go to the art museum."

"Worry about your son," he murmured under his breath.

"Hey!" She gave him a look. "All parents worry about their kids. It's perfectly normal."

"Hmm," he said, though his expression had

gone sad. For the second time that day, she wondered why.

"Do you have children?" she asked again. He didn't wear a ring, but that didn't mean anything.

"No." The word was bitten out, harsh and brittle and full of pain. She'd obviously hit a nerve there. Before she could say anything more, however, their ride approached. In the distance, a canvas-covered flatbed truck rattled along, with two women and a man already clinging to the steel poles in the back.

Gabe stood, ending their conversation. The vehicle stopped nearby in a cloud of dust, and after a nod from the driver, he stepped onto the flatbed, then held out a hand to help Sara up beside him. She gripped the nearest pole with both hands to avoid getting jostled when the vehicle started moving again.

Matteo and Doreen perched on a tower of hay a little way down, and Noah grabbed a free spot on the other side of the truck bed. The driver hit the gas, and Sara wound her arms around the pole, pulling her body and face close to the metal.

Gabe put a hand above hers on the pole. "Okay?"

"I think so."

"If you relax your muscles, it will be easier. Sara?" He leaned in closer to be heard over the roar of the engine and the wind. "This might get a little bumpy on the way down. Do you want me to ask someone to trade places with you?"

"No."

Then the truck picked up speed, and without thinking she reached behind her to grab him and pull him even closer to her, using him like a human seat belt as her hair whipped against her face and his body slid behind hers. Her heart pounded so hard, she was sure everyone in the truck could feel it, and by the time they reached the compound again an hour later, her knees felt so wobbly all she wanted to do was get in her bed and stay there until the next morning.

Gabe helped her down, and she mumbled her thanks before hurrying inside like the coward she was. Because unfortunately, her knees weren't the only thing wobbling now. Her conviction to keep her distance from Gabe was on shaky ground, too. And that scared her far more than any height or bumpy joyride ever could.

CHAPTER FOUR

THE FOLLOWING NIGHT, they all ate together in the dining hall at the dorms, cafeteria-style. Several local women from the nearby village cooked for them during the clinic trips, and tonight was homemade tamales, stuffed with veggies, plantains and cheese and spiced with plenty of garlic, the ever-present rice and beans, and *tres leches* cake for dessert. Yummy and filling after a busy day.

Gabe chatted with Noah and Matteo while Sara and Doreen sat a few feet away, talking quietly. He'd been impressed with Sara today, pushing through her jitters and stumbles with the language to do her work well. He admired competency. Admired compassion even more. And it hadn't escaped him how kind she'd been with the patients today.

They usually got new volunteers in each month, and Gabe had been doing these trips a long time. Over twenty years, all over the world. He'd worked with hundreds of nurses and doctors and other health-care professionals. Yet he'd never been as aware of one of them as he was of Sara.

He didn't want to think about why.

Not that it mattered. He wasn't a relationship kind of man. He'd tried that once, with Marija, and look how that turned out. They'd died, his wife and son, because of him, and he never wanted to go through that again.

"I'm sorry. What?" Sara asked Matteo, her light, happy tone jarring Gabe out of his dark thoughts.

"He asked you and Doreen what you guys are doing spending your free time at the hospital instead of a resort at the coast?" Noah translated with a grin.

It was something Gabe had wondered himself, though he wouldn't ask. The less he knew about Sara Parker, the better. Because the more time he spent with her, the more intrigued he became—whether he wanted to be or not.

"Tell him I don't do well with water. Get seasick," Sara said.

"Tell me yourself," Matteo answered with

a wink. "I speak English fine. Just messing with you. And what about Blondie?"

Doreen raised a brow at him, one side of her mouth quirking up. "Resorts are only fun with company. Are you volunteering?"

Matteo laughed, his teeth white against his tanned skin. "Not yet, *gringa*. But give me time."

The conversation continued on, Noah and Tristan joking and Matteo and Doreen bantering back and forth. Gabe's attention kept returning to Sara, though, who sat quietly now, poking at the remains of dinner on her plate.

"Filled up?" he asked at last, for lack of anything better to say.

"Yes. This was really good." She sighed, looking about as exhausted as he felt. "I'm just tired."

"How are you finding the work so far?"

"Busy, but good. Some things are different than back in Chicago, but a lot is the same, too."

"Like what?"

"The chaos."

Gabe chuckled. "I see. And you don't like the chaos."

"It's fine. I mean, I'm used to it, but my instinct is to control it." She shrugged. "Sometimes that isn't always possible."

"No, it's not." He looked at her from under his lashes again. Despite being out here in the rain forest, her clothes were pristine, not a wrinkle or stain on them. Even her hair, all those red curls he'd seen the day before yesterday ready to tumble everywhere, were now tamed to within an inch of their life into a neat ponytail at the nape of her neck. Yep. Everything about her screamed control freak, and yet all Gabe could feel was an insane urge to muss her up—run his fingers through those curls and free them, see if they felt as soft as they looked, rumple up those clothes of hers with his hands while he kissed her silly and...

Dammit. No.

He did flings. Nothing more now. And Sara Parker practically had a neon sign flashing *forever* above her head. He should stay away. Far away. And yet he found himself asking, "How about a short walk around the compound before bed?"

"Okay. Sounds good." Sara put her napkin on the table, then stood. "See you guys tomorrow."

Everyone said their good nights, then Gabe walked outside with Sara.

As evening drew closer, the temperatures dropped, but it wasn't chilly yet. A nice breeze rustled the trees around them, and the vivid colors of sunset were just beginning to stain the sky. They strolled in silence for a while until Gabe notice her peering into the foliage beyond the fence. "What are you looking for?"

"Spider monkeys, like Don Juan." She smiled in the gathering shadows. "Or sloths, maybe. Pretty much anything cute and furry that doesn't want to eat me."

"Do you like the rain forest?"

"Yeah, I do. Not that I have much to compare it to, though. I've never been camping."

Gabe scowled. "Camping?"

"You know. Sleeping outside in a tent and stuff. This is my first time."

"Huh. Well, the dorms aren't really outside, but I see what you're saying."

She chuckled.

"What?" he asked, frowning.

"Nothing. It's just your accent is stronger tonight."

"Really?" He shook his head. "I don't even notice anymore."

"Noah said you're from Croatia? How long since you've been home?"

"Long time. Thirty years almost," he said, then quickly changed topics. He didn't discuss the past with anyone, especially this woman, who seemed to slip under his skin without even trying. "Tell me more about this camping."

Sara hesitated a moment, as if she wanted to argue, then continued. "Well, there was this one time when I was eight and I went to Girl Scout camp. But it doesn't count, because we slept indoors then, too, in cabins."

"Girl Scouts? The ones with the cookies?"

"Yep." Sara grinned in the orangish glow of a streetlight. "I was the top cookie seller every year in my troop."

"How many years was that?"

"One."

He laughed. "Wait. Why only one, if you were the top seller?"

"Because my dad said I could only do one after-school activity at a time back then, and the next year I wanted violin lessons, so…"

"Ah." Gabe adjusted his longer stride to her shorter one. "So, you play the violin, too?"

"No." She shook her head and winced. "I was horrible. After the first round of lessons, the teacher sent me home with a note that he couldn't keep taking my dad's money."

"Wow. That is bad." He gave Sara a side glance and caught her spectacular smile, and damn if his chest didn't squeeze tight, stealing his oxygen. He really needed to keep his distance from this woman. She was far more dangerous to him than any gang or disease. Desperate to shift his awareness away from how those freckles of hers danced across the bridge of her nose, he searched for another subject that didn't involve him giving in to his weird need to get closer to her whenever she was around. He was in his fifties. A widower, for Christ's sake, not some hormonal teenaged boy.

"Want to work on your Spanish some more?" he asked.

"Uh…okay."

"Tell me what words you know so far."

"I don't know."

"You do not know what words you know?" He frowned, confused. "Okay. How about I'll say something in English, and you repeat it back in Spanish, yes? It's how I learned English in Croatia. Well, that and watching lots of TV and movies."

"Okay."

"Hello," Gabe said.

"Hola."

"My name is Sara."

"Mi nombre es Sara."

"Where is the bathroom?"

"Donde es el baño?"

He shook his head. *"Esta.* But in an emergency, that's okay."

"Donde esta el baño?" Her accent made the word sharp, but they were understandable.

"Good. You've got all the basics down." He grinned. "Bet you didn't know I'm a master teacher as well as an awesome doctor, did you?"

She fiddled with her already perfect ponytail as twilight descended. "The mystery deepens."

"Mystery?" Gabe frowned.

"About you. I can't figure you out."

"There's not much to know," he said, shaking his head. "Trust me. Nothing worth knowing, anyway."

She sighed and stared at the streaks of pink and orange fading into indigo in the sky. "I doubt that, but I know a brush-off when I hear one. Fine. Teach me more words."

Without thinking, he reached out and pressed a finger to her forearm, the light pressure making her velvety, reddened skin go white. "Sunburn."

"No clue."

"Quemada."

Sara snorted then repeated it.

Gabe blinked at her, imagining her tangled in his sheets, her cheeks pink and her eyes bright as she snuggled naked against him, those pink lips of hers swollen from his kisses.

Oh, God.

Swallowing hard, Gabe turned away and started toward the ward tent beside them. "I need to check on one of my patients before we head back to the dorms for the night."

Sara tagged along behind him, her sweet floral scent making his guilt even worse. What the hell was he doing out here flirting with this woman? He had no business doing it. Relationships were not for him. After Marija and his son had died, he'd tried to move on. Tried making it work with a new woman, but in the end his issues from the past had ruined it.

So, now, he never started. Just one-night stands and short flings where both people knew the score.

That's it.

That's all he deserved.

Sara deserved more. He didn't really know her or anything about her, but he could already say for certain that she deserved more than he could give. Because something deep and important had died inside him along with family that day in Vukovar, and he doubted it could ever return again.

"How many patients do you typically keep in the ward?" she asked as they entered the tent. Two rows of beds lined the walls of the long rectangle, and the air was filled with the sound of monitors beeping and the smell of antiseptic. Volunteers wove between the beds, checking vitals and making sure the patients were comfortable.

"We have capacity for up to twenty, if needed," he said as he strode to the end of the tent where little Chuly and her mother were staying. The last time he'd checked, the woman's vitals were better and her fever had gone down. Her bleeding had also stopped, and Gabe was hoping to wake her up tomorrow and perhaps discharge her by the end of the week. Chuly was up when they got there, playing with her dolls on her bed. Gabe crouched beside her and smiled. "*Hola*, Chuly. How is your arm tonight?"

"Better," she said, focusing on her toys instead of him.

"What are you playing?" he asked her in Spanish.

She told him how her dolls were on opposite teams, both trying to find a hidden treasure. "Like in the pirate movies."

"Ah." Gabe chuckled, all too aware of the prickling warmth on the nape of his neck from Sara's stare. "My son used to play similar games with his toys when he was your age."

"You have a son?" Chuly blinked at him with wide eyes.

"I did."

"What happened to him?"

"He's gone now," Gabe said, swallowing hard against the lump in his throat and the war-torn images flashing in his head. Even all these years later, it was so hard to talk about. *"Ahora vive con ángeles."*

"Oh." Chuly's attention was on her dolls again. "That's sad."

"Sí." Gabe cleared his throat then straightened. "I brought a friend with me tonight. Her name is Sara. She's a new nurse here at the hospital."

"Hola." Sara smiled and waved, though it

was clear she had been taking in what he'd just said.

"*Hola.*" Chuly squinted at Sara's red hair. "*Su cabello es rojo. Ella es una bruja?*"

Gabe laughed.

"What did she say?" Sara frowned.

"She wants to know if you're a witch because you have red hair."

"Oh. Well, not usually, but I do have my moments." Sara grinned. "At least that's what Luke says."

"Hmm." Gabe turned away from the little girl to check on her mother, who was still resting peacefully. "He sounds like a wise man."

"Beyond his twenty-one years." Sara moved in next to him, her arm brushing his and sending a riot of unwanted awareness through his nerve endings. "What's wrong with this patient?"

"Dengue fever. She had a lot of pain from internal bleeding when she came in, so I sedated her to allow her to heal in comfort. If her vitals stay good tonight and her fever doesn't return, I'll wake her up tomorrow and release her."

"That's great." Sara glanced back over her shoulder. "Is she Chuly's mother?"

"Yes." Gabe finished listening to the woman's breath sounds, then checked the lymph nodes in her neck. Honestly, he'd have danced a jig on his head if it gave him a distraction from the nearness of Sara. God. Why the hell had he thought walking with her tonight then bringing her here with him was a good idea? He hadn't been thinking. Or thinking with the wrong body part. That was the problem.

He'd been alone too long. That was it. On his next day off, he'd head into the nearest city and find some company for the night. Take the edge off. All these odd reactions to Sara Parker would go away and he could continue on alone, as he preferred.

Then he straightened fast and collided with her. Gabe reached out to steady her, and damn, her skin felt like velvet to his touch. She blinked up at him with those warm copper eyes and those pink lips of hers parted and her gaze flicked to his mouth and if he leaned in just a little bit closer, then...

Stop!

The word clanged in his head louder than the warming bells on the church in Vukovar the day the bombs had dropped. An ice-cold bucket of guilt and grief poured over his head and froze out everything else.

He let her go fast, like he'd been burned, and stepped back, throat tight. "We should get back to the dorms before the mosquitoes get bad. *Buenas noches*, Chuly."

"So…" Sara said, following him back to the tent exit. "I'm sorry to hear about your son. How did he die?"

The words stopped him short. He didn't talk about the past to many people, and certainly not nurses he'd just met, no matter how attractive. The black hole of grief in his gut, seared around the edges, raising his hackles. He looked away from her and mumbled, "The war."

"In Croatia?" she said, blinking up at him. "That must have been awful."

That was the understatement of the century. But how did you explain the devastation, the desolation, the utter annihilation of an entire city filled with people to someone who'd never been through it and would never comprehend what you'd been through?

You didn't. That was the answer. At least Gabe didn't, anyway. He just buried it all down deep and kept going day after day, because what else was he going to do? He had his work. That's what he was here for. That was his purpose now.

He took a deep breath, then sidled around her to head outside. "Excuse me, I need to get to bed. Busy day tomorrow."

Gabe walked out without waiting to see if Sara followed. They were right across the road from the dorms. She would find her way. He, on the other hand, felt as lost and broken as ever.

CHAPTER FIVE

EARLY THE NEXT MORNING, Sara stood in a stall in the shower tent, trying to wake up and trying to work through everything that had happened with Gabe the night before. He had a son and that son was now dead. Her heart broke for him. If anything happened to Luke, she wasn't sure how she'd cope with that.

But honestly, the man drove her nuts. She prided herself on knowing others well, on being able to anticipate their needs before they had to ask for things. And yes, her controlling, perfectionist side was showing, but she'd learned to accept herself a long time ago. After splitting from her ex, those tendencies were the only thing that kept food on the table sometimes. She'd owed it to her son to look out for him.

Okay. Fine. Luke complained now that it was time to stop, but still. Change was hard.

What was even harder, it seemed, was finding some privacy in the compound.

From the stall next door, Doreen was rattling on about something. As her roommate, Sara loved her new friend but had quickly learned to tune the woman out when needed to keep her sanity. Doreen was the kind of extrovert who needed to talk things out to find her answers. Sara was the opposite, turning problems over and over in her analytical mind until she found a solution.

Both ways were valid if opposite approaches to life. Both ways caused headaches of their own.

She scowled and squirted a dollop of shampoo into her palm. Her curls were so thick and feral with all this rain forest humidity that it felt like washing a bush sometimes. In the stall beside hers, Doreen continued talking about her TV show and the clinic and Matteo. Doreen talked about the clinic's dentist a lot. Sara was starting to think there was a crush developing there, at least on Doreen's side. She hadn't spent enough time with Matteo yet to know what he was thinking.

"Sara," Doreen whispered through the white plastic barrier separating them. "How are things with Gabe?"

"What?" Sara quickly rinsed her hair to keep the shampoo from running into her eyes, then turned to face the tent wall behind her. God. Was her interest in the man so obvious to everyone? If so, she needed to change that, quick. As casually as possible, she said, "Fine, I guess. Why?"

"No reason," Doreen said then chuckled. "Just seems you two work together a lot in the clinic."

"Huh?" Nose scrunched, Sara rinsed off her face then opened her eyes to find herself level with the small flap meant to help keep mildew from forming on the plastic stalls and discovered that they had a clear view to the other side of the tent, where the men's showers were. Whoops. She looked away fast. "Well, I don't think that means anything. He probably calls on me because I'm sitting in his direct eye line. That's all. I'm sure he doesn't mean anything by it."

"Sure. Okay." Doreen sounded less than convinced. "What do you think of Matteo?"

Sara shrugged then slathered conditioner on her parched curls. "He seems nice enough. I don't know him that well yet."

"He's very nice," Doreen agreed. "And single, too."

"Right. So you like him?" She smiled and shook her head. If anyone was conspicuously spending more time together lately, it was those two. And not just in the clinic, where they'd taken up exam spots beside each other at the opposite end of the tent from Gabe. "I think you'd make a nice couple."

Doreen's laugh echoed in the air. "Don't jump the gun there, missy. We're just friends. It's nice getting to meet new people again after…" Her voice trailed off. "Anyway, I think if there's sparks between you and Gabe, there's nothing wrong with that. That's all I'm saying. Go for it."

Heat prickled Sara's cheeks that had nothing to do with the sun beating down on them. She opened her mouth, but the words caught in her throat. She'd actually dreamed about him last night—the two of them tangled in her sheets, working up a sweat that had nothing to do with the temperature outside…

But no. She wasn't here for that. She wasn't looking for love anymore. She was here to make a difference.

Except she couldn't stop thinking about the hurt, haunted look in his deep green eyes last night when he'd mentioned his son. *He's gone now.* Ahora vive con ángeles. *He's with the angels*. And what about a wife? Was Gabe still married? He didn't wear a ring, but that didn't mean anything.

Maybe it was the caregiver in her, but she wanted to know more about him. The pain in his expression drew her in like a moth to a flame. One of the reasons she'd gone into nursing was to help people during the most difficult times in their lives. To ease their way through to the other side. Deep down, she sensed a wealth of heartache inside Gabe, and she longed to help him.

Of course, the control freak in her wanted to steer far away from the doc, because her reactions to him never followed any of her rules. Yet there was something about the man that kept drawing her back in, kept drawing her closer, kept her wanting more...

Doreen snorted. "And don't think I don't see the way you melt every time he looks at you, Nurse Parker."

"I do not melt," Sara snapped.

"Oh, yeah. There's definite goo inducement happening there." The sound of Doreen's shower curtain sliding open echoed through the space. "Not to mention your sappy expression whenever he's around, all soft and kittenish."

"I'm not kittenish," Sara grumbled as she finished rinsing off, then grabbed her towel to wrap around herself before exiting alongside Doreen. "And I don't have a thing for Dr. Novak. We have to work together on this trip. I'm just trying to be cordial."

"Cordial. Uh-huh. Sure." Doreen rolled her eyes. "Well, whatever you call it, I've got eyes. And the times you're not looking at him, he's looking at you, sweetie. That's way more than cordial in my book."

Sara straightened from where she'd bent over to towel dry her curls, blinking at Doreen. Was that true? Did Gabe watch her? There'd been times, in the clinic, when she'd have sworn she could feel his stare on her, but she'd put it down to silliness. But maybe it wasn't so silly after all...

No. Forget it. Didn't matter. No matter what kind of odd attraction thing might be happening between them, she wasn't here for it. Best to steer clear from now on and leave things as they were. Besides, she was only here a month. Then it was back to Chicago and life as normal.

There was no space in her world for a romance with the gorgeous Dr. Novak. Long-distance relationships never worked, and he was obviously invested in this place.

But what about a fling, though?

That thought stopped Sara in her tracks. It must've shown on her face, too, because next thing she knew, Doreen chimed in again.

"Love is in the air in Costa Rica, eh?" the other woman laughed.

"What? No." Sara finished drying off then pulled on fresh clothes quickly.

"Why? You like him. And from what I've heard from the other guys, he could use some TLC."

Her mind returned to last night in the ward with little Chuly. He'd been so open with the child, so vulnerable and had looked so heart-breakingly lost when he'd mentioned his son.

And she'd learned her lesson with her ex— don't force your assistance on people who don't want it or deserve it. Gabriel Novak might deserve her help, but he'd made it clear he didn't want it. The end.

Except she kept remembering how he'd pulled her close the other night after dinner at Alma's, how his tall, muscled body had felt against hers, the brush of his warm, strong fingers on her skin, and damn.

That had been…well…*something*.

Not that she was dwelling on it. Nope. Not at all.

Sara brushed it off to her friend as best she could.

"We're coworkers trying to get along in the clinic, that's all." At Doreen's skeptical look, she turned away to slip her feet into her flip-flops. Gah! What a mess. There was no reason the tall, dark and broody head doc should make her feel more like a giddy teenager instead of the wise forty-two-year-old she was. No reason her heart should race, and her chest should squeeze whenever he was near. None. And yet, they did, regardless of Sara's wishes. She shook her head, repeating out loud her thoughts from earlier for Doreen and the world to hear. "Anyway, I'll be gone in a few weeks, so it doesn't matter. And I'm here to work. Period. Not to mention, we just don't click."

"Click?" Doreen had ditched her fake eyelashes and the rest of her makeup and looked a whole lot younger without them. "How do you know?"

"You just know. Not to mention every time I ask him anything personal, he shuts me down. Seriously." She waved to the rain forest around them. "We're too different. He's out here in the middle of the jungle saving people, and I'm back in Chicago trying to decide what to do with the rest of my life. It makes me feel…" She swallowed hard, searching for the right word. "Insignificant."

"Hey. None of us are insignificant." Doreen shrugged, shimmying back into her clothes then braiding her wet hair. "If life has taught me anything, it's that we all have our own paths to walk. Don't judge someone else until you've worn their shoes. I'm sure you make a real difference in your PICU in Chicago, and I'm sure they miss you while you're here." She gave a sad chuckle.

"A lot of people think I'm nothing but a preening airhead because of that reality TV show. Some even accuse me of not being a real doctor. But it doesn't matter what they think, because those are real people I'm helping on the show and real skin diseases I'm treating. I'm getting the word out about the science behind the medicine, and we reach a global audience. No way I could have that kind of influence sitting in my small practice at home. And sure, I might have to dress up like a diva for the ratings, but that doesn't make my message any less true or real."

Sara took that in a moment, seeing her

friend in a whole new light. "No, I guess it doesn't."

"Damn right it doesn't." Doreen hooked her arm through Sara's and tugged her back into a shower stall. "Now I'm off to brush my teeth."

"Have fun."

Doreen waved as she walked out of the tent.

Sara finished towel drying her curls then pulled them back into her usual neat ponytail at the base of her neck before leaning back into the stall to collect her bottles and soap. The move put her at eye level with the ventilation flap again, and without thinking, she glanced out and froze at what she saw—Gabe beneath the water, all glistening tanned skin and gleaming muscles, nothing left to the imagination. His broad shoulders rippled as he shampooed his dark hair, then lathered up his face to shave. She couldn't stop looking at him or the trail of white suds slipping down his sinewy back to the curve of his lower back. Nor could she keep from wondering what it would be like to trace that line with her fingers—maybe her tongue, too. Her mouth went dry, and her breath hitched.

Oh, God.

"Uh-huh. Strictly cordial, my ass," Doreen said, popping Sara's lust-filled bubble.

Flustered, she turned fast to face her friend. "I wasn't peeking. I reached in to get my stuff and the flap blew open and..." She exhaled slow, praying her dirty thoughts weren't written all over her face and knowing they were. "It was an accident, that's all. And why are you spying on me? I thought you were brushing your teeth. That's not fair."

"Neither is love, sweetie." Doreen locked arms with her, and they walked out of the tent together. "But it's not supposed to be. Love is meant to teach us, to help us grow, to make us the best versions of ourselves. Fairness doesn't usually play into any of that."

Sara nearly stumbled over her flip-flops, feeling loose and wobbly and entirely off-kilter. "When did you become a love guru?"

Doreen laughed as they headed back toward the dorms. "Stick around, kid. I'm just getting started."

Dusk was falling by the time Gabe finished with his last patient in the clinic. It had been a busy day as always, filled with lots of routine aches and pains, a few broken bones and lacerations. He cleaned up his area, then headed across the ward to check on Chuly's mother. He'd had the techs reduce her sedative earlier because she'd improved so much. If all checked out well, he'd send them home early.

But when he entered the ward tent and headed to the far end, he saw that Chuly and her mother weren't alone. Instead, Sara sat on Chuly's bed, playing dolls with her while the mother watched, smiling. His gut tightened at the vision of them so happy and carefree. He couldn't remember the last time he'd felt that way himself.

After a deep breath, he walked over to them. "How're my patients this evening?"

"*Mucho mejor ahora,*" Chuly's mother said.

Much better now.

"Glad to hear it." He stared down at the top of Sara's lowered head. "And how's Nurse Parker?"

"Good," she said, not looking up from the doll in her hands. "Just spending some time playing."

"Hmm." Gabe got busy checking the mother's vitals a final time instead of standing there, grinning like an idiot at a woman he had no business wanting. "Everything sounds good," he said to the mother in Spanish. "Any more bleeding or pain today?"

The mother shook her head.

"*Buena.*" He jotted down his findings in the patient's notes, then looped his stethoscope around his neck. "Well then, I believe you are done here. I'm discharging you from clinic tomorrow morning."

"*Muchas gracias,*" the woman said, hugging him around the waist before smiling. "*Hora de acostarse*, Chuly."

"*Por favor, ¿puedo quedarme despierto hasta más tarde, mami?,*" the little girl asked.

"No, Chuly. You need to get your rest tonight for the walk home tomorrow." Gabe crouched beside the bed, far too aware of Sara watching him. "We need this space for other sick people. But I promise, the next time you come back, I'll have a special treat for you."

"*Si?*" Chuly gave him an incredulous look.

"*Si.*" Gabe's smile widened. He remembered his son, Karlo, getting that same expression when he was trying to bargain for more toys or treats. It was a bittersweet memory that made his heart ache with grief and yearning. He straightened then and picked up Chuly, spinning her around to stand next to her mother and making her giggle. Sara gath-

ered up the girl's toys into a plastic bag and
handed them to Chuly. "Now, *buenas noches*.
Both of you."

He left them to settle in for the night and
walked out of the tent with Sara, aware of her
watching him curiously.

"What were you thinking about just then?"
she asked.

"About getting them home so I can get to
dinner."

She sighed and shook her head, standing,
mumbling something under her breath he
didn't quite catch.

"I'm sorry?"

"I said you are locked up tighter than Fort
Knox."

He scowled. "What is that?"

"Fort Knox? It's a big vault in the US where
they keep the gold reserves."

"Ah." Gabe resorted to teasing to steer
away from the thudding of his heart and the
race of his blood due to her nearness. "So,
you're saying I'm a treasure."

"What? No." Sara frowned, crossing her
arms. "I'm saying you're locked up tight. Impossible to crack open without the right com-
bination. Infuriating."

She looked so adorable, all flushed and

furious, eyes sparkling and cheeks pink, that without thinking Gabe reached out and brushed a curl that had escaped her ponytail away from her face, his finger tracing the line of her cheekbone before pulling away. They were standing close, far closer than he'd realized. So close that if he bent his head slightly, he could kiss her, feel her warmth breath on his skin, taste those pink lips he'd been dreaming about for days.

No. Stop it.

Chances were good he'd ruin this like he ruined everything else when it came to personal relationships. He'd fail Sara just like he'd failed his wife and son.

But what if it's not a relationship? What if it's just sex?

Thunder rumbled in the distance, and Gabe closed his eyes, ignoring the flashbacks of the bombs and sirens clanging in his head, the rubble of Vukovar as he'd climbed through the debris to rescue Marija and Karlo, only to find them already gone. It should've been him. There were times, too many times, when he wished it were…

"Hey," Sara said, her quiet voice bringing him back to the present. "You okay?"

Gabe blinked down at her for a small eternity as his temples throbbed and sweat prick-led his skin. Then, slowly, the cool breeze and birdsong helped anchor him to the here and now. Sara's hand was on his arm, and he counted the freckles across her nose to calm his raging pulse.

Eventually, they wandered outside, where the last streaks of sunset had stained the horizon pink and blue and gold. In front of the dorms, Matteo had started a small fire in the fire pit and was roasting fish that one of the villagers had caught in the river that day and brought to the clinic as thanks for treatment. He and Sara settled on a log across from Matteo as the sky above turned to black velvet scattered with a thousand flickering white stars.

He ignored the looks Matteo gave him as he passed Gabe and Sara dinner, his mind still whirling with the fact that somehow, some way, this woman affected him like no other in a long, long time. Worse, all of a sudden he now seemed to be considering the idea of sleeping with her. It was a solution that would certainly scratch the annoying itch of lust he felt whenever she was around. But only temporarily, and only if she agreed to the affair and the same rules. No emotions. No string attached.

They'd have to discuss it first, but they weren't anywhere close to that yet. The chemistry between them was off the charts whenever they were in close proximity, sure, but it was complicated. Besides, there'd be plenty of time to see how things developed, if it developed. They hadn't even kissed yet. The residual adrenaline still sizzling in his veins was making him get ahead of himself.

Budala. Fool.

Low blood sugar. Yep. That had to be it, why he was thinking such crazy thoughts tonight, why he'd almost kissed Sara in the ward tent. And the cure for that was food.

So, for now, he relaxed and enjoyed a nice meal with his team.

There'd be plenty of time for worries and recriminations tomorrow, if his past was any indication.

CHAPTER SIX

HIS INDICATIONS ABOUT the past were wrong,
at least as far as having time to talk to Sara
about...well, whatever this thing was between
them. Because the next day was even busier
than the day before.

Clinic started out routine enough, with
exams and vaccinations and such, but then
the village midwife showed up, and things
went downhill from there.

Valentina fluttered around Gabe, pelting
him with details about her patient's progress-
ing labor in rapid-fire Spanish. Her face grew
redder with every syllable, and she pressed
on her stomach as she spoke. Around them,
patients waited, trying not to listen in, but
with the crowded quarters, it was impossible
not to, really.

"I'll come as soon as I get my things together," he said, putting his hand on the wom-

an's arm to comfort her. "You go stay with her now and try to make her as comfortable as possible."

The midwife scurried out of the clinic, glancing over her shoulder at the doorway, her dark eyes pleading. "It's my daughter. Please hurry."

Gabe nodded, then went over to speak with Noah. "Can you handle these four patients left? See if Doreen might help? None of them appear to be bleeding, broken or teetering on the brink of death, so I think you'll be okay."

"Sure thing, Doc," Noah said. "We got it covered. Go deliver that baby."

"That's the plan." He hated letting people down, so he always strove to do the best he could and persevere despite their circumstances. It was a lesson he'd learned well back in Croatia. "I'm taking Sara with me, just in case."

"Good call."

"Where is she?" He dropped his supply bag on the bench.

"Outside with the kids, I think." Noah hiked his chin toward the open space beside the tent. "Said something about a game or something."

Sure enough, he found her in the grass with

a pile of scuffed metal jacks and blue rubber ball in front of her, surrounded by a circle of local children. Gabe walked over, and the kids froze at his arrival, squinting up at him in the sunshine. "I need your help. Breech birth."

"Sure thing." She stood and dusted off her scrub pants. "Do you need me to bring anything special?"

"Just your PICU experience." As they zipped along the path between the houses, Gabe filled her in on everything he knew thus far. "The patient is seventeen, first pregnancy. Not due for another four weeks, but the midwife—her mother, Valentina—said the patient's water broke this morning. She's certain the baby is breech. I'll examine her to determine dystocia then first try to turn the baby in utero. If that doesn't work, then we'll need to get her standing and try the McRoberts maneuver. You know it?"

Sara nodded. "I didn't work on the OB floor, but I did a rotation there during nursing school."

"Good." Gabe smiled, impressed. "Talk me through it. To be sure we're on the same page."

She did. "Hyperflex the thighs to widen

the pelvic outlet. Apply suprapubic pressure to rotate and dislodge the anterior shoulder. Avoid fundal pressure, because it could worsen the condition or cause uterine rupture. Then insert a hand into the posterior vagina and press the posterior shoulder to rotate the fetus in whatever direction is easier. Biggest risk is compression of the umbilical cord during delivery."

"Excellent." They stopped in front of a one-story white stucco house. A crowd of about ten people were gathered on the front lawn, their hushed voices doing little to drown out the patient's screams from inside. As soon as Gabe and Sara started up the path to the front door, the people surrounded them.

"She's in so much pain," one woman whispered to Gabe in Spanish.

A man with a scraggly beard shook his head. "This sounds very bad."

"Lo tengo."

I've got it.

He pushed back the length of fabric over the door frame, and another scream slashed the air. He looked back at Sara over his shoulder, his blood thumping so hard he felt it in his toes. "Ready?"

"Yep." Sara followed him into the house,

where a rotund man greeted them in the front room. Valentina's husband, Roberto. He clapped Gabe on the back, then ushered them down the hall to where the patient, Angela, waited. A single, narrow window provided the only source of light in the room, and the air inside felt at least fifteen degrees hotter than the rest of the house. On the bed, Angela panted, her face scrunched in pain and her damp black hair plastered to her forehead. Beside her, Valentina looked at Sara as if she were an alien species.

Sara gave Gabe a side glance. "Are you sure she's okay with me being here?"

"It's fine. Valentina is the village midwife, and she's understandably nervous and protective of her daughter Angela, the patient." Gabe pulled on a pair of gloves, then knelt next to the bed.

Sara followed suit, moving in beside him. "What do you need me to do?"

"Palpate her abdomen, please. Tell me what you feel."

She did so, pressing her fingers into the girl's midsection. "Something hard and smooth. The baby's head. It's here." She kept pressing. "And an elbow or knee here. Yep. Presentation is definitely breech. Hard to tell if it's frank or complete, though, without an ultrasound."

"Good. Okay. I'm going to try and flip the baby," he said to Valentina in Spanish.

But three hours, dozens of contractions and numerous tries later, Angela was fully dilated but still breech. All his attempts to turn the baby had failed, and resignation hung heavy in the room.

"What now?" Sara asked. "C-section? Seems risky this far away from the clinic."

"You're right. It is too risky. We need to prepare for a breech delivery." He straightened, peeling off his gloves. "Can you go ask Roberto for blankets, please?"

"Absolutely." Sara started out of the room then stopped. "How do you say blankets in Spanish?"

"*Mantas.*" Gabe glanced up from his supply bag. "Hurry, please."

"Be right back."

While he waited, Gabe washed his hands with bottled water and Betadine, then pulled on fresh gloves before laying out the instruments he might need during the birth, including a scalpel and a syringe filled with lidocaine for Angela's episiotomy.

Finally, after what seemed like forever,

Sara returned with an armload of blankets and a huge slice of ripe mango in her mouth. At Gabe's raised brow, she finished chewing and swallowing the fruit then plopped the blankets down next to the bed. "Roberto said I looked thirsty, so he stuck the mango in my mouth. What next?"

"Get fresh gloves on while I handle this." He knelt at the end of the bed and first used the syringe to numb the area, then cut the episiotomy with the scalpel. The scent of copper and sharp antiseptic filled the air. He looked up at Angela, then her mother. "We need to get her standing and then squatting. Sara, can you hold Angela up, please?"

Sara rushed around to the girl's head, hooking her arms under Angela's and planting her feet wide as she and Valentina heaved the patient into a squat.

"Good. Now we push." Gabe looked up at Angela, the front of his scrub shirt stained with sweat and blood. "On the next contraction, I need you bear down hard." Then to Valentina and Sara, "You'll have to hold her steady."

Angela whimpered and squirmed.

"Push, push," Gabe and Valentina chanted.

"We have one leg. I'll try to bring down the other on the next contraction."

The girl writhed and grumbled, and three pushes later, he'd managed to deliver the baby's arms. Valentina wrapped the half-born infant in one of the many blankets Sara had brought in as Angela cried out once more.

The biggest problem with breech births, other than the umbilical cord, was the head was the largest part. In a usual birth, the head widened the cervix for everything else. But in a breech birth, the head came last, making it all more difficult.

Sure enough, with every push, it became more and more obvious that his hands were too large for the job.

Damn. Just damn.

Gabe waited for the current contraction to end, then turned away, cursing under his breath.

Sara left Angela resting in her mother's arms for a moment and walked over to him. "What's happening? What's wrong?"

He kept his gaze averted, afraid she'd see what he tried so hard to keep hidden—the terror, the doubt, the knowledge that the one time he was needed the most, he'd been unable to save the lives of those entrusted to his care. This situation was like reliving the worst day of his life. Like being back there in that apartment in Vukovar the last day, debris strewn everywhere, the acrid stench of explosives and death all around him. Him trying and trying to make things right but failing over and over and over again. Guilt weighed heavy on his chest, cutting off his oxygen. Asking for help wasn't his strong suit, because life had taught him that too many times, help arrived too late. It had in Vukovar, for his wife and son.

"Hey," Sara said, shaking his shoulder. "Talk to me. I'm here to help, remember?"

Help. She was here to help.

Gabe hazarded a glance up at her and saw the determination in her pretty face. Perhaps this time would be different. Wasn't like he had much choice, anyway. "I need you to deliver the baby."

"What?" Her eyes widened. "Why?"

"Because your hands are smaller than mine and Valentina's. You must reach inside and ease the head out of the birth canal. Otherwise, we'll lose them both."

"But I've never done that before."

He met her eyes then. "I know. But we're

out of options. She's too far along to move at this point."

For a moment, Sara looked like she wanted to argue, but then she nodded. "Okay. Talk me through it."

Pride in her pinched his heart. He knew the courage it took to face the unknown and do it anyway.

Above them, Valentina cooed to Angela, rocking her from side to side, whispering low while her dark eyes remained locked on Gabe, a warning in their depths. *Let my daughter die and you'll soon join her.* Gabe recognized that sentiment and vowed to do everything he could to save both Angela and her baby.

Bolstered by Sara's steely conviction, Gabe felt firmly grounded in the present again. He tried to give her the quickest, most concise explanation of what needed to happen during the delivery, but between the exhaustion and strain, it emerged in a mess of English, Croatian and Spanish.

"Sorry," he said, taking a deep breath. "I'm probably not making much sense."

"It's okay." Sara moved in beside him. "Let's do this step by step. That'll be easier for everyone."

"Okay. First, reach into the birth canal and find the baby's face."

She did, wrinkling her nose in concentration as she worked. "Okay. I feel the neck."

"Good. Reach farther."

"And the chin… I think."

"Find the baby's nose. You'll have to reach past the cervix."

Her lips compressed, and she closed her eyes. "What will it feel like?"

Gabe frowned. "Like a nose."

Sara shot him a look over her shoulder. "Gee, thanks."

"Sorry." He exhaled slow and pulled back the blanket to point at the baby. "I mean it will be on the underside. See how the toes are toward the ground?"

She nodded and closed her eyes again, the taut silence broken only by Angela's intermittent moans and the jackhammer of Gabe's heart in his ears.

"Got it!" Sara grinned.

"Great." Relief washed through him, making his shoulders sag forward a bit. "I'm going to have her push. Keep your fingers around the nose so the head does not turn to the side. Keep it straight and guide the face down with your hand. I'll work on the rest of the body."

Angela whimpered, and Gabe glanced up to find tears streaking Valentina's face. He'd never seen the midwife cry. Not once, and they'd been through numerous difficult births together over the years. But this wasn't everyday work. This was her daughter.

He knew better than anyone the power of family and what that kind of loss did to a person.

"One more push, Angela," Gabe said. "Push with everything you have."

The girl let out a deep, guttural moan, and the infant's body moved downward a fraction of an inch. Angela slumped against her mother, taking a portion of the progress they'd made with her.

Sara stood then moved to the head of the bed, forcing Angela to meet her eyes as she said to Gabe, "Tell her I felt the baby's face and he has fat little cheeks." Angela gave a weak smile, and Sara continued. "Now tell her we need her to push one more time. Tell her she can do it. For her son."

Gabe translated the words, and Angela gave a small nod.

"Okay." Sara moved back into position. "I've got the nose. Let's do this."

Angela bore down hard, grunting as her mother chanted in her ear.

One minute later, the baby boy let out his first cry.

CHAPTER SEVEN

AS THEY WALKED back to the clinic, Sara marveled at the lush foliage. Everything seemed bigger now, brighter now, since the birth. She still couldn't quite believe she'd done that. Working in the PICU, she cared for tiny infants all the time. But bringing them into the world? Now that was something.

The late-afternoon sun filtered through the trees, its rays still prickling Sara's sunburned skin as they passed a bar, a crowded convenience store and a school painted in primary colors in the village. Gabe pointed toward a tiny house to their left. He looked rumpled but perfect, a tiny, infant-size handprint staining the front of his scrub shirt. "That's where to go for the best tortillas in Costa Rica."

"Really?" Sara smiled. "I'll have to remember that. Thanks for letting me help out today."

"Thank you for being there," he said, the solemnity in his green eyes making her think they were talking about more than the breech birth.

Before Sara could ask more, however, they reached to compound and walked back to the clinic tent to drop off their supplies. At the entrance, an older woman waited, her gray bun perched precariously atop her head and her blue cotton dress neat but faded a bit around the edges.

"*Hola,*" Gabe said, waving. "What can I do for you?"

The woman smiled, then spoke in rapid Spanish.

"Anything I can help with?" Sara asked him, setting her supply bag on the table inside the tent.

"*Sí.*" Gabe grinned, walking past her to his exam area to drop off his stuff. "She's inviting our team to dinner tomorrow."

"Oh." Sara straightened. "That's very nice."

"It is." He chuckled. "She's an old friend and a patient here at the clinic. She feels it's her duty to feed us while we're here."

The woman, still waiting at the entrance, nodded. She spoke to Gabe once more, too fast for Sara to keep up. Maybe something about a horse? Or hair? She could never keep those two words straight. Gabe moved in beside Sara then, and maybe it was the adrenaline from earlier still sizzling through her veins, or the joy of bringing new life into the world. Whatever it was, she suddenly couldn't help being aware of how close he was standing behind her and how if she leaned back just slightly, his chest would rest against her back, all warm and solid and...

Oh, boy.

Gabe promised the woman they'd all be there for dinner the next evening, and the woman walked away, leaving the two of them alone again. Inside the tent, long shadows increased the intimate feel of the moment.

"Thanks again for your help with Angela," he said, leaning in to rest his free hand on the desk behind her back. Her body buzzed, hyperaware of his every move even though there was still a good foot of space between them. He lowered his head and stared at the ground. "There were moments during the delivery when I thought..." His dark brows drew together.

Cicadas sang their nightly song outside the tent, but inside it was just the two of them. Sara hesitated, then asked the question that had been on her mind since she'd arrived and first met Gabe. "What happened to them? Your family?"

He swallowed hard and straightened, and for an awful second, she thought he might shut her out again, but then he took a deep breath and said quietly, "They died. When our apartment in Croatia was bombed during the war. I lost my family, everything I cared about within a matter of hours."

"Oh, God." Sara's own heart broke at the eviscerating agony in his voice. "I'm so sorry, Gabe."

She tried to put her hand on his arm, but he took a step back, reaching into the back pocket of his scrub pants for his wallet. "I have a picture of them. Would you like to see?"

Sara nodded, trusting herself not to cry.

The photo he pulled out was a bit crinkled and bent at the edges, as if handled a lot. He moved closer to Sara again, handing her the picture, then pointing at the pretty woman smiling in it. "Her name was Marija. We were married almost two years when this was taken. She's holding our son, Karlo."

Blinking back tears, Sara smiled. "She's lovely. And Karlo is precious."

"Thank you." He took the photo from her, staring down at it reverently. "He was our everything. We couldn't wait to move from Vukovar to Prague and start a new life there, but I had to finish medical school first. Marija and I used to fight about it, but she let me win." He gave a sad little snort. "I was so young and stupid back then. I thought we'd have all the time in the world."

"You couldn't have known this would happen," Sara said, touching him now to emphasize her point. "No one knows what the future holds."

"I should have." His expression darkened to a scowl, and he put the photo away, those damned walls of his crashing down hard again. "Anyway, I apologize if I seemed distracted during the delivery earlier."

It took a moment for his words to penetrate the emotional fog in Sara's brain. "You weren't distracted. I thought you were brilliant today. You saved them both, Angela and her baby."

"No, you did." Gabe smiled again, and it felt like a million stars shining to Sara, that dimple of his making her slightly dizzy with yearning. "Without your small hands, all would have been lost."

Sara held her hands up as she shrugged. "Genetics, I guess."

"Hmm."

The low whirr of the generators kicking on outside reinforced the fact that she and Gabe were still alone out here in the tent, standing in the shadows, so close that the heat radiating from his skin penetrated the thin cotton of her scrubs, sending her pulse skyrocketing.

"We should probably go into the dorms," she murmured past her taut vocal cords.

"We probably should," he agreed.

Neither of them moved.

Finally, Gabe reached into one of the drawers of the nearest table and handed her something.

"What's this?" she asked, staring down at the chunk of cellophane-wrapped white in her palm.

"Sweets for the sweet. *Dulce de coco,*" he said, his teeth even and white as he smiled in the darkness. "Coconut candy. I get tired of eating beans and rice."

She sniffed the stuff. "Wow. Smells amazing."

"It's very good." Gabe stood there a moment, staring down at her, then sighed and turned away. "Well…uh… I guess this is good night, then." He started to leave, but Sara placed a hand on his forearm, her fingertips tingling from the touch. Gabe froze, looking back at her, his green eyes flicking from her eyes to her mouth, then back again. Her name emerged low and rough, and she felt it like a physical caress. "Sara?"

"Yes?"

Silence stretched for eons. Finally, he stepped closer once more, his fingers trailing down her arm, firm but tentative. Gentle but wanting. "I want to kiss you, but I know I shouldn't."

He was probably right—she knew that. With his past and her future waiting back in Chicago, getting involved, even temporarily, made no sense. And yet, at that moment, Sara wanted to kiss him more than she wanted her next breath. Taking the initiative, she closed the small distance between them and wrapped her arms around his neck, pulling him down until their lips met. She put all of her whirling emotions into it—the sweetness of the birth, the sadness of his picture, the need and want she'd felt for him since the first day she'd met him. Gabe seemed taken aback at first, holding back, but then her tongue traced his lips, and he gave in with a grunt, pulling her tight against him as he deepened the kiss. His mouth was perfect against hers, mirroring the soft eagerness of his touch. She couldn't help giving a desperate whimper.

More. I need more.

The sound of footsteps outside the tent finally jarred them back to reality.

Sara inched away, breathless and light-headed.

Gabe's warm breath fanned her face, stirring the tiny hairs near her temple. He gave a short sigh full of frustrated need, then kissed her forehead. "Tomorrow we talk, yes?"

"Yes," she whispered, savoring the feel of him against her while she could.

"Good." Then he brushed his lips across her forehead and started for the exit again. "Sleep well."

She waited a moment, catching her breath and calming her racing heart, then headed for the dorms herself. Sara wasn't sure about a lot of things, but having a restful night after a kiss like that would be impossible—of that she was certain.

CHAPTER EIGHT

GABE FELL ASLEEP dreaming about kissing Sara and woke up thinking about the same. The way her body had felt pressed against him. How wonderfully her mouth fit his. The velvet feel of her skin and the softness of her moans.

He made his way to the door, careful not to wake his roommate, Matteo, who lay sprawled across his bed, a paperback with a cracked, worn spine perched open on his chest. The minute he stepped out into the hallway to head to the latrines and showers, though, he came face-to-face with a rumpled and adorable Sara, the early-morning sun filtering in through the windows dancing off her loose, tangled curls.

"Hi," she whispered, glancing at him, her gaze a tad groggy.

"Good morning." He smiled back before

realizing he hadn't brushed his teeth yet. "I, uh, was on my way to the bathrooms." He held up his towel and toiletries kit.

"Me, too." She pointed to the tote bag slung over her shoulder. He didn't look too long at her pink tank top or flowery bottoms and how they clung to her petite curves. Nope. Not at all.

"Shall we walk together?" he asked.

"Sure."

The awkwardness was strong this morning as they walked side by side out of the dorms and into the already hot and humid air.

For lack of anything better to say, Gabe asked, "How'd you sleep?"

"Okay." Sara shrugged then swatted a curl out of her eyes. "There's no clinic today, right?"

"Right."

"So, what do we do then?"

"Hang out. Relax. Sometimes we get a football game going. Or I think you Americans call it soccer."

"Oh." She wrinkled her nose. "I've never played."

"It's fun. We'll teach you."

"Okay." She took a deep breath, then raised her face to the sun, eyes closed. "I should probably do some laundry, too."

"You could come to breakfast first with me at my friend Carlos's house," he said, then wanted to kick himself. What the hell was he thinking? He never brought women along on his visits, but there was something about Sara. Somehow, she'd slipped beneath his walls. God, he'd even shown her a picture of his family. He hadn't shown that to anyone since Janice. And that hadn't turned out well at all. It was the only serious relationship he'd tried to have since leaving Croatia, and Janice had just pushed too hard, too fast, wanted things from him that he couldn't give. Things he wasn't sure he'd ever be able to give again—like his heart, his soul, his forever.

For many years, he'd thought those things had died. But the more time he spent with Sara, and now after yesterday and kissing her last night, he'd begun to wonder if maybe, just maybe…

And maybe you're getting senile in your old age, glupan.

Gabe snorted and shook his head, dodging a large rock in the road as they turned the corner to the latrines and shower facilities.

Dumbass was the correct word for how he felt these days. Like he wasn't sure if he was coming or going, just sticking to his routine and his mission trips because what else was he going to do with his time?

Now, though, he began to think that perhaps there was life beyond these mission trips, a world he'd left behind years ago, that perhaps he could rejoin if he wanted to. Until a few weeks ago, he'd had no interest in that, but that breech birth yesterday had made him stop, made him think…

"Who's Carlos?" Sara asked, squinting up at him, shielding her eyes with her hand.

"He lives in the village. His wife passed away a few years ago, and he raises his daughter alone."

"Oh." She seemed to consider that a moment. "Well, I guess I could, if you don't think he'd mind an extra guest."

"He won't."

"Okay. I'd love to go with you, then."

Two hours later, they were on their way. The village bustled with people doing their morning chores. Customers shopping. Farmers tending to their livestock and chickens. Children running off to school in their uniforms, laughing and shouting.

"Hungry?" Gabe asked as they wove through the crowd. Many of the villagers recognized them and waved as they passed. "Carlos makes a mean breakfast."

"Yes, I'm starving," Sara said, her damp hair pulled back in a tight braid. "Unless it's beans and rice. Please tell me it's not beans."

He snorted. "It's not beans and rice. Or, at least, not all beans and rice. You like eggs?"

"I do," she said, grinning.

The crowd grew, and without thinking, Gabe took her hand to keep them together. Then he kept it, because it just felt so good to touch her. Usually, he didn't linger with any of the women he slept with, avoiding unnecessary signs of affection. He'd forgotten how something so simple could make him feel so good. The fact Sara didn't pull away made him feel even better. "Come on. It's this way."

They turned a corner and traversed several side streets in silence as Sara took in the town. At first, he tried to be discreet, sneaking a glance or two her way as they walked. But as they got closer to his friend's house, Gabe gave up all pretense and looked at her all he wanted. By the time they arrived at Carlos's, he felt both unbalanced and elated, like a schoolboy all over again.

His friend stood outside his one-story white

stucco home chopping wood while his five-year-old daughter collected eggs beneath their chicken coop nearby. It was a lovely property with a small wood behind the house that abutted the Rio Frio river.

"Gabe!" the little girl called, giggling.

He scooped her up and tickled her sides as she held tight to the egg in her hand, squirming enough to scare the chickens back into their roost, at least until she spotted Sara.

Gabe lowered the girl back to the ground and spoke in quiet Spanish. "Esme, this is Sara. She works with me in the clinic. She's a nurse."

Wide-eyed, Esme stared up at Sara.

"*Hola*, Esme." Sara crouched beside the girl and waved. "How old are you?"

"*Cinco!*" Esme held up that many fingers.

"*Cinco? Dios mío.*"

Esme giggled again, then handed Sara the egg she'd cradled before taking Sara's other hand and pulling her into the thick cover of trees on the back of the property.

"What is this, my friend?" Carlos asked, waggling his brows at Gabe. "You never bring them here."

"I know. And before you start, she's just a friend."

A friend you'd like more from.

He shook his head, not ready to explain things between him and Sara. Not sure he even could at that point. Hell, they'd only kissed once, and yet she'd somehow found a way past his barriers without even trying. Gabe shrugged. "Nothing's going on."

"Looks like something to me." Carlos snorted, and Gabe scowled. "Relax, *muchacho*. I won't embarrass you. Too much."

Gabe ducked away from the house, the scent of rain forest and heady flowers surrounding him as he searched for Sara and Esme. Under a thick cover of branches, he found Sara cross-legged on the ground, eyes closed and hands folded around a half dozen or so eggs in her lap, while Esme fiddled with Sara's braid. The girl put a bright pink ribbon around the end of it, then frowned, shook her head, and switched it to purple and green instead. Then Esme stomped her foot and started again.

"Forgot to mention Esme is a world-renowned hairstylist, didn't I?"

Sara smiled and opened her eyes. "You did."

"*Muy bien*, Esme." Gabe picked up Esme again. "Time for breakfast."

* * *

After they devoured a hearty, delicious feast of plantains, eggs and tortillas, and spending an hour or so catching up with his friend, Gabe and Sara started back toward the compound.

"If you want to visit longer with Carlos, I don't mind," Sara said. "I like Esme."

Three women sat on a front porch across the street, and Gabe waved to them. "No, I think Carlos has told you enough embarrassing stories about me today."

Sara laughed. "Are you sure? I still have some questions about the pregnant eighty-year-old-woman."

Gabe shook his head and kept walking. "To be fair, it was my first visit to this village, and the people here tricked me into believing it was true."

A couple of loose chickens raced past them, squawking, and Sara moved closer into his side, her arm bumping his as she took his hand again. He should let her go, push her away like all the others, but damn if he could.

"Where now?" she asked.

"Well, if you want to put your laundry off a bit longer, we could stop at the market." Gabe greeted a man carrying a basket of corn who passed them.

"My dirty clothes can wait." She grinned. "Is this just to browse or is there something you need?"

"Nope. Just for fun." Feeling lighthearted and free for the first time in recent memory, Gabe laughed and tugged her along.

As they walked back into the heart of the village, they came to a tattered blue length of rope hung across the road. Drooping in the middle, it hit Gabe at the knees. To one side, a uniformed police officer sat inside a small hut, watching, a sleek black rifle leaning against the wall near his feet.

Gabe waved to the man before stepping over the rope.

"Are we supposed to…" Sara frowned, gesturing toward the guard.

"It's fine. You can step over."

"Then why is he there?" She looked at the guard again, who watched them over his newspaper.

"It's a stopping point. To search trucks coming through from Nicaragua to make sure they're not smuggling people in."

"And they think a piece of rope will stop a

truck?" Sara scowled. "All it would take is a strong pair of scissors."

Gabe shrugged and let her go, his hackles rising. "They do the best they can with what they have. Not all countries are rich like America."

She winced. "Sorry. I didn't mean—" Sara stopped. "That sounded dismissive and judgmental and privileged in all the wrong ways, and I shouldn't have said it. I was trying to be funny and obviously wasn't."

Gabe stopped and looked down at her. "It's okay. We all say and do things we don't mean sometimes. I suppose I won't send you back to the compound in shame." His frown dissolved into a grin. "This time."

They continued on to a pink two-story building. The ground level was wide-open, and two small boys stood on the balcony above. People wandered about, arms loaded with baskets and plastic bags.

"How many vendors are in here?" Sara asked.

"Depends on the day. Locals all come here to sell their wares," he said as they shuffled inside. "Everything from produce and livestock to pots and clothing."

The interior was dim after the sunshine,

and the smells of smoky chili peppers and spices hung heavy in the air. Stalls and racks of goods crowded every available space, and the din of bargaining created a constant, dull roar.

Sara immediately located a display of American snack chips and picked up a bag. "Uh, I think I need these, but there's no price tag."

"Nacho flavor?" Gabe made a face then plucked a different bag from the rack. "Cool ranch always."

"We can agree to disagree." She grabbed both kinds and headed for the counter. "And I'll get both. Because I'm nice."

Gabe rolled his eyes, grinning again as he leaned in and kissed her forehead. "Very nice. But you also need some Fanta Roja to go with that."

"Fanta what?" Sara frowned.

"Red pop." Gabe reached into a nearby fridge and pulled out two red cans. "It's king in Costa Rica."

Then he deftly took the bags of chips from her hands and stepped up to the counter before she could stop him. Nisha, a lean, leggy girl with wide eyes and flushed cheeks, waited on him. He recognized her from the village, and she smiled and talked in Spanish as she rang up their stuff, then tucked it all into a plastic bag. Sara stayed quiet beside him.

On the way back to the compound, she finally broke her silence. "So…"

"So?" he asked, his gut tightening a bit and the space between his shoulder blades knotting. Last night, he'd told her they needed to talk today, but he'd been putting it off. Mainly because he wasn't sure what to say. Normally, when he approached a woman about having a fling, it was in a bar, and they were both a bit drunk, making it easier. But with Sara it was different because…well, dammit— everything with her seemed to be different. Gabe wasn't sure why and didn't want to look too closely at it at this point for fear of ruining it. So, he stalled for time. "What did you think of the market?"

"It was fun," she said, staring straight ahead. "Is the cashier a friend of yours, too?"

Gabe glanced sideways at her. "No. I mean, we chat and things when I'm in town, but I wouldn't call her a friend." Gabe took Sara's hand again and squeezed. "What's on your agenda this afternoon? Besides laundry. And chip eating."

His joke went over like a lead balloon, apparently, because she didn't laugh.

Instead, Sara stopped and faced him. "Look, Gabe. I know we're both still working through that kiss last night, and that's fine. But you should know that the reason my ex and I divorced was because he cheated on me. Repeatedly. Now, I know there's nothing between us yet and there's no guarantee there will be, either, but if you've got something going on with that cashier or with someone else at the compound, I'd like to know now before things go any further."

Right. So much for avoidance.

"I have not slept with that woman, nor do I plan to," he said. "For starters, she's half my age. And secondly, no. There's no one I'm involved with that way at the compound. Believe it or not, I don't usually go around kissing my coworkers."

Pretty pink stained Sara's cheeks, and she stared down at her toes. "I'm sorry. I didn't mean to get all personal with you like that."

"Too late." He chuckled, then tugged her closer to kiss her forehead. "Besides, sticking your tongue in my mouth is way more personal than that question you asked." He sighed then stepped back to meet her gaze.

"I like you, Sara. I don't know where this will lead between us, but I'd like to spend more time with you while you're here. I won't cheat on you, because I don't do relationships. That's something you should know up front. But while we're together—" he took a breath "—if we're together, it will be exclusive on my part. On yours, too, I hope."

"Oh, well…" She blinked at him a moment, and Gabe's heart sank. Maybe he'd gone too far, too fast. Maybe he'd blown the whole thing with her before it even started. Better that, though, than get too invested and get shattered into a million pieces again. Then she stepped forward and kissed him again, and it was every bit as good as he remembered from the night before and then some.

He couldn't get enough, pulling her closer and taking control, tasting her, holding her, stroking her soft, warm skin. Apparently, Sara couldn't get enough, either, if the fact she was trying to climb him like a tree was any indication. Her words from before swirled in his head.

The reason my ex and I divorced was because he cheated on me. Repeatedly.

Gabe didn't know the bastard, but what an idiot. Any man who'd cheat on a woman like

Sara had to be the biggest dumbass in the universe.

Finally, she pulled away as several villagers on the road around them cleared their throats and laughed.

Whoops.

They both composed themselves, then hightailed it back to the compound, hand in hand. Once they got back to her room in the dorms, Gabe tossed their bag on Sara's bed, then grabbed one of the cans and opened it for her before handing it to Sara. Laughing, she took a sip, the sugary, red soda fizzing out the top.

"Good?" Gabe asked, wishing he could lick the sugar from her lips. But there were too many people around right now. When he took Sara, he wanted her all to himself.

"Yes. I haven't had one of these in years. My son, Luke, used to love them, though." She set her can aside, then reached up to cup his jaw, now covered with a slight shadow of stubble. "Really good."

Gabe swallowed hard, the soda burning his throat as it went down. Maybe one more kiss wouldn't hurt anything. He quickly closed the distance, pulling Sara in for another deep kiss, savoring the berry sweetness coating her mouth. He couldn't get enough.

"Sara—" he started, pulling back slightly, but she was having none of it.

She pushed him down to sit on the edge of her twin bed, then straddled him, her thighs bracketing his as she kissed him long and hard and deep, slipping her tongue between his parted lips. He rocked up into her, unable to help it, he wanted her so much, his hands tracing her spine, letting her know he wanted her as much as she wanted him. Finally, she came up for air, easing back enough to gasp. "How are we going to do this, then?"

Leaning his forehead against hers, their panting breaths mingling, Gabe whispered, "What?"

Then he was kissing her again, the softness of her lips driving his need higher. It had been so long, too long. She slipped her hands under his shirt, running her fingers along the smooth skin of his back, his muscles bunching beneath her touch. She whispered, "The fling."

"Oh," he murmured against her lips, nuzzling the spot beneath her ear that made her shiver as his fingers slipped beneath the hem of her shirt and traced up her abdomen, heading for her breast. "Well, I think we have a pretty good start here already."

"*Hola.*" Doreen's voice broke through their tangle of passion, and Gabe groaned, burying his face in Sara's shoulder. Would he never get to have this woman?

Doreen continued on as if nothing was happening. "Don't mind me. I just need to grab a few things from my bag."

Sara rested her chin on his shoulder, motionless, her heart pounding in time with his.

"Worst timing ever," Gabe whispered in her ear, making Sara laugh as Doreen continued to putter around on the other side of the room. Finally, Gabe sighed and moved Sara off his lap to stand. "I need to do some things in my room, if you'll excuse me." He stopped at the door and looked back at Sara, all pink and perfect and still panting from his kisses. "We'll continue this later."

CHAPTER NINE

THAT NIGHT, AFTER finishing a game of soccer with the local kids to burn off some excess frustration, Gabe picked up the ball and declared it a tie. His opponents weren't happy, but he needed to get ready for dinner. He'd promised the team would go to dinner with one of their patients this evening. Her name was Barbera, and she was one of their nicest patients.

He turned to walk back to the dorms as the crowd dissipated and spotted Sara sitting on a bench near the fence, reading. He hopped the fence and walked over to stand behind her, bending to kiss her neck and loving the way she shuddered under his touch.

"Sounds like they want to keep playing," she said, turning slightly to look up at him as she closed her book.

"I promised them a rematch tomorrow."

His mind kept replaying the way her hips had shifted against him as they'd kissed, how she'd arched into him earlier. He wondered if anyone would notice if they skipped dinner and sneaked back to the dorms for more alone time. Those ideas were banished quickly, however, when three of the local boys ran up to the fence, still sweaty from soccer.

"Gabe! Gabe!" they called, stopping short at the sight of Sara, lanky, awkward machismo only teenaged boys could pull off. The gawked openly at her, irritating Gabe to no end, while she just waved and smiled.

"You have *novios*." he said. "Boyfriends."

Sara snorted and shook her head. "That's taking cougar to the extreme."

He glanced at the fence again, where the boys now dangled their arms and legs through the gaps.

"*Hola,*" the tallest one said. His hair fell over one eye, and he pushed it back every few seconds. "I'm Ary."

"*Hola*, Ary." Sara leaned over to shake his hand through the fence. "How old are you?"

"Sixteen," Ary said, though Gabe knew for a fact he was only thirteen. He raised a brow at the kid but didn't correct him. Sara smiled wide, and given how fantastic her legs looked in those shorts, Gabe couldn't blame the boy for trying.

"Brothers?" she asked, pointing at the three of them. They nodded, quick and eager.

"You have brothers?" Ary asked.

Sara shook her head. "How do I tell them I'm an only child?"

Gabe told them for her, and the boys went nuts. Hands fluttering and weaving in and out of the fence as their words morphed between broken English and fluid Spanish.

At Sara's curious look, Gabe said, "Being an only child is unusual here."

"Oh." She stood, wrapping her hands around the fence post and smiling as she talked to the boys. They pelted her with questions, some in Spanish, some in English. Sometimes she understood and answered, sometimes Gabe translated, always wishing they'd leave so he could have her to himself. The boys wanted to know everything, it seemed like. Her parents' names—John and Linda. Her birthday—February 3. Her favorite color—purple. Whether she liked Shakira. Gabe would've told them to stop, but he wanted to know all those things, too, so he let them keep asking.

"*Te gusta melocotón?*" Ary asked.

Sara glanced up at Gabe, clearly confused.

"He wanted to know if you've ever tried…
I think you call it star fruit," he said.

"*No sé,*" she told the boy.

Ary scrambled up the fence. At the top, his
arms gave out, nearly impaling him on the
sharp edges. He tumbled to the ground, then
brushed his pant leg off and tried again. This
time he made it over, muscles wobbling. He
dropped to the ground then pulled himself up
tall, and Gabe and Sara parted to make room
for his teenage ego.

"*Vamos? El árbol de melocotón?*" The kid
bounced on his toes with excitement.

"There's a star fruit tree near his house.
He wants to take you there," Gabe translated,
praying she'd say no. The trip would leave
him no time to kiss her again before they had
to leave for Barbera's house.

"Is that okay?" she asked Gabe. "I mean,
there's enough time and all, right?"

He sighed then nodded. "Yes. We'll be back
in time." Ary watched them with anticipation
from beneath his shaggy hair, so Gabe put the
kid out of his misery. "*Vamos.*"

Ary linked arms with Sara, and Gabe followed beside them. His younger brothers scurried on ahead of them. They walked out of the
gates of the compound and toward the village,

then veered off on a side path that wove between houses and climbed a few stairs.

Finally, they arrived at a tall, slim tree, and
Ary let go of Sara's arm to circle the thing.
Dappled late-afternoon sunlight dotted the
ground around them, filtering through the
leaves. Then, after two complete loops, the
boy chose a spot and snaked up the trunk.
His long legs and feet gripped the bark, and
he yelled down to Sara, asking if she could
see him. She shielded her eyes, shouting en-
couragement. The other boys called out, too,
guiding Ary to the closest fruits.

With a thud, the boy came down from the
tree and walked toward them. His hands were
raw from the climb, and he clutched the hem
of his shirt into a pouch for his spoils.

"Look!" He revealed four yellow fruits. He
handed the biggest, ripest one to Sara and
the smallest one to Gabe. His brothers took
the last two, leaving Ary empty-handed. He
yelled after his brothers and waved a fist in
the air, but they were already gone.

"Here." Gabe handed his over to the kid. He
wanted to save his appetite for later anyway.

Ary nudged Sara. "Try it, try it."

She gave Gabe a bewildered look. "How
do I eat the thing? Do I need to peel it first?"

"No. Just eat it." He gave her a look. "They don't have these in your grocery store?"

"Maybe." Sara shrugged. "But I'm more of a berry girl myself. You know… Strawberries, blueberries. Blackberries, mulberries. Pretty much anything you can put in a pie."

Ary nudged her again. "Try it."

"Okay, okay." She laughed and took a large bite from the middle of the star fruit. Juice ran down her chin, and Gabe wanted nothing more than to lick it off her. "Wow! That's really good. Very, very good."

Indeed.

"Time to go," Gabe said, steering Sara back toward the compound. "We don't want to be late for Barbera's."

Sara waved to Ary over her shoulder. *"Adiós, amigo. Gracias por la…"* She looked over at Gabe.

"Melocotón."

"Melocotón," she repeated.

Ary nodded, smiling wide as he caught up to them and took Sara's arm again, walking them all the way back to the compound.

They arrived at Barbera's house about fifteen minutes late that night, mainly because Gabe kept stopping on their way to the village to pull Sara in for a deep kiss, and she came utterly undone.

"We should hurry," she said when he finally pulled back slightly, her breaths shallow.

"Eh, Barbera always runs a little late anyway." He shrugged, kissing her again, softer this time. She raked her hands along his chest, loving the solid heat of him. "We'll be fine. Come on, *dušo*. It's just around the next corner."

When they arrived at the home, Barbera came up and gave Sara a kiss on the cheek and a hug before showing her around her small two-bedroom home. In the kitchen, Sara was surprised to find Doreen darting around in a yellow apron over her T-shirt.

"What's up, guys?" she said when Sara walked in with Gabe, holding up a wooden spoon. "Barbera made me the sous chef for the evening. Cool, right? And FYI, we're not allowed to open the fridge, because Noah's extra insulin is in there and he needs it to stay cold."

"Where is Noah?" Sara asked, trying and failing to wrap her mind around Doreen as June Cleaver. The air smelled of roasting meat and veggies and also something sweet in the oven. "What are you making? Smells fantastic."

"It's a surprise, but you'll love it," Doreen said, grinning.

Gabe's warm, solid hand pressed against Sara's back, the weight of his palm inching past the waistband of her shorts, and Doreen's words faded as her concentration zeroed in on his touch. "Great. Cool. Can't wait." She pulled Gabe out of the kitchen and outside to a steep set of wooden stairs. At the top was a balcony that overlooked the village. Homes climbed the rolling hills beyond the road, and on the horizon streaks of color remained from the glorious sunset.

"Lovely," Gabe said, but his eyes never left her face as he trailed a finger down the length of her neck.

Her eyes fluttered closed, and when she opened them, he held out a hand to lead her to a hammock strung in one corner of the balcony and pulled her in after him, snuggling her into his side. "I've been waiting for this all day."

"Me, too." She leaned into him, holding him tighter, listening to the steady pound of his heart beneath her ear. "I'm glad you're here with me now."

"Hmm." He kissed the top of her head and pulled her closer atop him. The thick rope dug into her arms, but she didn't mind. There wasn't anywhere else she wanted to be right then, the feather-soft cotton of his T-shirt caressing her cheek. "What will you do when you go back home?"

Sara lay there a second, thinking. "Well, there's my son, Luke. But he's in college now out in California, so I don't see him as much as I used to." She took a breath. "I've got a few days after I get back before my sabbatical's over, and there're some projects around the house I want to work on. And there's a new Renoir exhibit coming to the Art Institute I'd like to see and…"

Before she even realized what was happening, Sara was crying, her face buried in Gabe's shoulder. He wrapped his arms tighter around her and squeezed, his chest muffling her sniffled. "What's wrong?"

"I don't know," she muttered, pulling back. "I guess I thought I'd come here and get some direction, some sense of where I wanted my life to go next, but now…" She shrugged, feeling stupid and raw and a tad guilty. "I just don't know. And…well. I miss my son. Luke and I don't talk the way we used to, and I'm lonely, I guess." Sara exhaled slow, smoothing her hand down Gabe's shirt. "I'm sorry. Didn't mean to be such a Debbie Downer."

"Who?" He frowned down at her.

Sara laughed through her tears, shaking her head. "Never mind."

"Okay, Debbie." He kissed the top of her head, his chuckle rumbling beneath her ear. "Should we go back inside?"

"In a minute," Sara said, snuggling closer, not ready to leave this moment—and his arms—yet.

The sun sank lower, and generators all over the village churned. The lights on the balcony flickered on. Without a word, Gabe reached over Sara's head and flipped them off.

"So, besides your projects and the art exhibit, what else will you do with your time?" he asked.

A rush of anxiety slithered into her chest. "Not sure yet. Maybe I'll go back early. Lots of people are probably off on vacation right now, so I'm sure the PICU can use me."

Beneath her Gabe shifted, and Sara looked up into his face. The sway of the hammock lulled her into a stupor, and all she could see was his rumpled, sexy look that made her blood sing. She rested her hand over his heart and her chin on top of it. "What about you? How long will you keep working here at the hospital? Is this where you see yourself in five years? Ten?"

Several beats passed before he answered, his fingers tracing absent patterns on her back as he spoke, his expression thoughtful. "Ever since Marija and Karlo died, I've kept busy, never stopping. I've never really questioned it until recently. But now I will be fifty-five soon, and I wonder if there's something more, something different, I should be doing. This hospital, this charity, they are good, but there's so much more that needs to be done." He took a deep breath and closed his eyes. "I don't know, either."

"Well. Aren't we a pair?" She propped herself up on her elbow to study him. There was a tightness to his mouth now, whether from stress or frustration, she wasn't sure. "A temporary one, anyway."

"Hmm." He opened his eyes then and smiled, dimple on full display. "I don't want to think about it tonight."

"No?" She leaned up slightly, bringing her mouth closer to his. "What do you want to think about?"

Fireflies flickered and cicadas sang around

them as his hands inched up the bottom of her shirt, grazing her hip. She slipped her fingers beneath the collar of his shirt to trace his collarbone. He shuddered beneath her, and Sara grinned. Her fingers moved upward, grazing an imaginary line from his shoulder to his jaw. Then she ducked and brushed her lips over his. "This?"

He growled and tugged her closer, nipping at her bottom lip. "*Sí*. This."

CHAPTER TEN

UNFORTUNATELY, THE NEXT day was busy, as was the entire rest of the week. Between clinics and patients and side trips to the village to make house calls, Sara didn't think she'd spent more than an hour in Gabe's company totally alone—though they'd sent plenty of longing looks each other's way. She dreamed about him at night, too, and her body still sang from the kisses and caresses they'd shared. For the first time in a long time, she felt free.

Free to choose what she wanted. Free to do as she pleased, without her control crows coming to peck at her happiness. And sure, maybe it was all just temporary, but wasn't Luke always going on at her to get a life? Well, here in Costa Rica she could have one, at least for the next three weeks.

For eleven years, she'd stayed in a loveless

marriage with a cheating liar, all in the name of giving her son a good life. But when Luke had started to pick up some of his father's bad habits in middle school, like lying to Sara about where he was going and who he was spending his time with, she'd realized that what children saw was just as important as what they were told. If she wanted her son to live a happy, healthy life, she needed to be a role model and live one herself. So she'd filed for divorce and hadn't looked back since.

Luke had turned out just fine. Sara liked to imagine this fling with Gabe would turn out just fine, too.

By the following Saturday, their next day off from the clinic, she was keyed up tighter than an overtuned guitar string, hoping they'd finally be able to continue where they'd left off at some point today.

But first, laundry.

She carried her bag of dirty clothes to the facility near the edge of the compound and got busy sorting lights from darks. Through the chain-link fencing, she spotted some local boys playing soccer in the relatively empty parking lot beside the compound. There weren't washers and dryers, since they were in the middle of the rain forest, after all. But there were several large, deep sinks with ample clean water tanks and clotheslines to dry your things on after they were clean.

She threw a pile of light-colored clothes and underthings into the nearest sink, then tossed a scoop of detergent over them before filling the basin with tepid water. Up to her elbows in suds, she scrubbed, swishing and swirling her items in her best impression of a washing machine. As she worked, a group of about ten boys gathered near the fence. She recognized a few of them from the last clinic and waved, water dripping from her fingertips.

"Looks like you have a fan club," Gabe said, hiking his chin toward the boys as he walked into the tent. It was probably Sara's imagination, but the air seemed to fizz whenever he was around. Or maybe that was just her bloodstream. "You should sing while you do that. Makes the work go faster."

"Uh, no." Sara laughed. "No one needs to hear that."

Gabe scoffed then nudged her over with his hip and a smile. "Everyone does it here. It's tradition."

He dunked his hands into the soapy water and came up with one of her T-shirts, rubbing the sides of shirt together hard and brisk while singing under his breath in what she assumed was Croatian. The tune was off-key and nothing she recognized, but soon Gabe was belting it out like a Vegas lounge singer. The boys on the other side of the fence laughed and pointed, mimicking his horrible dance moves.

Sara couldn't stop laughing. She took the now-clean shirt from him and hung it on the line to dry, then turned back to find him holding up one of her bras. Cheeks hot, she quickly hip checked him out of the way and took over again. "I think I got it from here. Thanks."

He chuckled and kept singing as he dried his hands, but between beats he leaned in behind her, his warm breath on her neck making her shiver. "Perhaps soon I will see you in that, *dušo.*"

Throat dry, she looked up at him over her shoulder, and time slowed. The world fell away, and it was just the two of them, his face so close she could see the tiny flecks of gold in his green eyes, smell his spicy scent, feel his taut torso pressed against her back. She swallowed hard and opened her mouth to say… Well, she had no idea what to say.

She wanted him, no doubt about it, but now wasn't the time. Not with the kids watching and other volunteers coming in to wash their clothes and…

Gabe kissed her temple then stepped back. "Finish your laundry. I'll distract them. We'll talk later."

Then he picked up a nearby blue soccer ball and threw it over the fence to the boys before vaulting himself over the top of it. He looked back at Sara, all lithe male confidence and sexy sinew, smiling and winking at her over his shoulder. And, oh, boy. Later couldn't come soon enough.

An hour or so passed before she finished washing all her stuff and hung it up to dry. Stiff and achy, she wandered out of the small tent to get some fresh air. It was late afternoon now, and the sky glowed pink and orange, giving her some reprieve from the sun's beating rays.

Beyond the fence, the soccer game continued. Gabe waved, and one of the boys nearby came over to her. He was tall and gangly, with spiky dark hair and a tiny scar bisecting his right eyebrow, giving him a perpetually skeptical look.

"Hello," he said to her in heavily accented English. "I am Lalo."

"*Hola*, Lalo." Sara smiled. "How old are you?"

"Thirteen," he said, grinning. "Would you like to play *fútbol*?"

"Oh, I don't think so. I'm not very good." She shook her head. She'd helped Luke practice back when he'd played in grade school, but it hadn't gone well. "You'd have more fun without me."

"*Vamos,*" Lalo said, gesturing to her to follow him toward the makeshift field. "Come on."

"It's fun, Sara," Gabe yelled to her from the parking lot. "Unless you're afraid I'll beat you."

She knew very well he probably would, but it would be nice to get some exercise. "Okay."

Lalo claimed Sara as his teammate, and within minutes, five or six more kids jumped into the mix. Then a few more. Before long, it seemed every child in the village had converged on the soccer game. The teams and the roles were informal, and after a half hour playing, Sara drooped under a layer of sweat from where she stood guarding the goal.

Gabe stood nearby, leaning forward to

rest his hands on his knees, pulling his black shorts taut across his tight butt. And yeah, okay. Maybe playing soccer did have a good point.

"Who's winning?" she yelled to him.

He shrugged. "No clue."

Then the kids were running toward them again, the ball flying in front. Gabe dived into the mix, stealing the ball and driving it toward the other goal. The younger kids squealed and laughed, but the older ones tore after him, intent on taking back command of the ball.

She watched from where she stood, too tired and hot to chase after them.

"Sara, look!" Lalo called and waved to her from the opposite end of the field. It was the third time in the last ten minutes he'd insisted she watch him. He was just like Luke at that age, all sharp angles and uncoordinated bouncing, and he never managed to make a play, but at least he was persistent.

She waved back and gave him an encouraging smile as he took off. Dust and flecks of mud flew up behind him, and Lalo kicked, completely missing the ball. Again. Except this time, he hit the ground hard, taking out a handful of kids with him.

Sara ran over to where Lalo had landed on his side, his knees curled into his chest as he cringed and moaned, holding his left shoulder. Gabe knelt beside him, examining him.

"How can I help?" Sara asked.

"Let's get him inside the ward tent," Gabe said.

Together they got the boy to his feet. It was obvious Lalo's left shoulder was higher than his right and that he kept that arm plastered to his chest.

"Fracture?" she asked Gabe as they made their way into the empty ward tent and eased Lalo onto the nearest bed.

Gabe rolled up the boy's shirtsleeve. "Dislocation."

Perspiration beaded Lalo's forehead, and a dozen tiny scrapes marked his elbow. A deep rivet sank into the skin just below his left shoulder. Gabe spoke to him in rapid-fire Spanish.

"He said this has happened before. Three months ago. His aunt pushed it back in the place," Gabe said. He wrapped a piece of tape around the boy's sleeve to keep it out of the way, then grabbed a nearby supply bag and dug through it. "If it happens once, it happens many times. He'll need to learn how to fix it himself. We'll do it this time, though."

"Sara can fix, *sí*?" Lalo stared up at her with wide brown eyes.

"*Sí*," Gabe answered before Sara had a chance. He held up a bottle of lidocaine in one hand and a syringe in the other, drawing a dose, then recapping the needle with the lid between his teeth. "But first, I need to numb the joint to make it less painful for you, *sí*? Plus, it will make the ligaments looser and easier to work with."

The boy's face went pale, and his gaze darted around the tent before landing on the exit.

"Hey." Sara put her hand on his good arm and flashed him a bright smile to distract him from what Gabe was doing. "It's okay. You know, when my son, Luke, was about your age, he broke his arm playing baseball. He had to get a cast and everything. He hated shots, just like you, but sometimes you have to be brave and do the hard things anyway. Can you do that?"

Lalo stared at her for a long moment, then gave a curt nod, his Adam's apple bobbing. "*Sí*."

"Good."

Gabe cleaned the boy's shoulder with an alcohol wipe, then leaned in with the needle. "Look at Sara."

Lalo's gaze locked on hers, and his grip tightened on her hand. He flinched for half a second as the medication went in, then it was over.

"Good job." Sara patted Lalo's hand. "I knew you could do it."

"We'll wait a minute for that to take effect." Gabe eased Lalo onto his back and palpated the dislocated shoulder, then glanced up at Sara. "You've reset an arm before, yes?"

"Yes," Sara said. "It's been a while, though."

"I'll talk you through it. Put one hand around his left wrist," Gabe said. "And the other on the forearm, just above the elbow." Sara did. "Good. Now keep the hand on his forearm steady and move his wrist very slowly ninety degrees. Like this." He demonstrated on his own arm. "If there is too much resistance or he's in too much pain, stop. Don't force it."

Her pulse thudded loud in her ears. "How will I know?"

"You'll know."

She gulped back a sudden rush of nerves

and rotated the boy's arm until it was at a right angle from his rib cage. "Now what?"

"Now place one hand on his bicep and lift like this." He raised his own arm above his head, keeping the elbow bent. "You'll feel the joint move back into place."

Sara inched the boy's arm upward and felt it jerk into place. She smiled. "Done!"

"Better!" Lalo started to sit up.

"Wait!" Sara felt the bone slide out of the socket again with his movements, and her stomach sank.

"Stay still." Gabe put his hand on Lalo's chest and forced him back down on the bed. "Try again. I'll hold him still."

The arm was harder to move this time, and Sara kept remembering back to when Luke had been in the ER with his broken arm. She looked over at Gabe and wondered if he'd had flashbacks like this during the breech birth, remembering the loss of his wife and child. Then she remembered how he'd told her about them, showed her that picture. How maybe he'd let her inside, at least a little. Her heart squeezed with tenderness.

Gabe held her gaze, his own eyes warm and encouraging. "Go slow. Pull out a little on his elbow this time. Don't jerk."

Sara did, but the arm wouldn't budge. She released the pressure and counted to five, then she tried again, pressing on the elbow while lifting the forearm, picturing the bone slipping back into the C-shaped joint. Finally, a dull pop sounded, and the pressure released.

"Better," Lalo said again, staying still this time.

"We'll make him a sling then walk him home," Gabe said. "I need to talk to his mother."

"Okay." She turned away to hide the weird urge to kiss him silly in celebration. "Do we have slings?"

"No. We'll need to make one from a shirt." Lalo asked Gabe something in Spanish, and Gabe scowled and shook his head. "No, no."

Confused, Sara looked between them. "What?"

Lalo glared at Gabe.

"He wants to make his sling out of one of your shirts," Gabe said. "To remember you by."

Sara laughed and stood. "Considering what happened today, that's the least I can do for him. Let me run to the laundry tent. Be right back."

* * *

The breeze was a welcome relief from the humid air inside Lalo's house. They'd spent the last hour packed into the living room as Gabe showed the boy's mother techniques to force his shoulder back into place. All the while, Lalo glued himself to Sara's side and rambled on about how she was the best nurse he'd ever seen.

Gabe couldn't argue. The boy was right. Sara was remarkable.

Night had closed in now as they slowly walked back to the compound hand in hand, light on their path coming from the windows of the houses along the main street and the full moon above. It wasn't the night he'd planned, but it felt right anyway. Good thing he'd planned ahead.

"Thanks for letting me fix his shoulder," she said, squeezing his hand. Shadows covered half of her face, but her copper eyes were still bright. "It's been almost twenty years since I did something like that."

"Thank you for helping. It's a two-person job, though I'm afraid Lalo will be heartbroken tomorrow when he wakes up and you're not there at his bedside."

"Whatever." She snorted. "I'm old enough

to be his mom. Hell, I'm almost old enough to be his grandmother, now that I think about it."

"Hmm. Well, you're the sexiest grandmother I've ever seen." He tugged her closer, then off the road and onto a footpath that curved away from the village and up a hill. The sweet fragrance of plumeria and star fruit trees drifted on the breeze.

"Where are we going?" she asked, the light of the full moon reflecting in her eyes as she looked up at him.

He couldn't resist stopping to cup her face and kiss her. It seemed like it had been years since he'd tasted her, and he couldn't get enough. Might never get enough. Somewhere in the back of his head a little warning bell niggled, but he was too happy and content at that moment to care. Gabe pulled back slightly then held up a finger, grinning. "Wait here."

Alone, he jogged the rest of the way up the hill to the clearing and grabbed the bag of things he'd brought up here earlier from their hiding spot behind a boulder. Quickly, Gabe laid out a blanket and pillows, two bottles of Imperial, a bag of Sara's favorite snack chips, and some chocolates he'd picked up at

the market in the village. Then he lit the cit-
ronella candles he'd brought and set them on
the rock surrounding his little love den before tucking the duffel bag away behind the
boulder again.

Gah! He had no idea what he was doing
with her, honestly. Usually, when he wanted
to sleep with a woman, he just put it out there
and they went back to his room. Or hers. But
this thing with Sara felt different. Not necessarily in a way he could explain, or wanted to,
but...different. And so he wanted to make an
effort to woo her. This was her first time in
Costa Rica, after all, and their first time together. Just because it was temporary didn't
mean it couldn't be special.

An exhilarating mix of nerves and excitement buzzed inside him as he headed back
down the path to where Sara waited for him.
He hadn't felt this way in years. Not since he
and Marija had been dating.

It was intense. It was intoxicating. It was
oddly fragile and strong at the same time.

He felt pulled in a million different direc-
tions at once tonight, but at the center was
Sara.

And with her, now, was the only place he
wanted to be.

Gabe stopped about a foot away from her, feeling younger and lighter than he had in years. Images of that frilly pink lace bra of hers from the laundry earlier that day flashed into his mind, and he couldn't wait to strip it off her with his teeth.

But first… "Close your eyes," he said, taking her hand again.

"What is going on?" she said, though she did as he asked, smiling.

He walked around behind her, wrapping his arms around her to guide her the short distance up to the clearing. At the summit he stopped and bent slightly to whisper in her ear. "Okay. You can look."

Sara blinked at his setup, and for an awful moment, he thought she might hate it. He was out of his element here. Out of practice. Out of touch. Out of time.

"Gabe," she gasped, turning in his arms to face him, her lovely eyes shimmering in the candlelight. "It's beautiful. Did you do this for me?"

That's when he knew things would be okay. Maybe not tomorrow. Definitely not in a few weeks when she was gone. But for tonight, for now, they were okay.

His breath rushed out, and he pulled her

close, rocking her back and forth, unable to stop smiling like an idiot. "I did this for us."

"Even better."

He forgot about everything but her in his arms, sliding his hands down to press her hips into his as he kissed her.

She swayed into him, making him shiver as her fingers slid into his hair. Fireflies glittered like stars around them, making it all seem even more magical. There was only now. Only the two of them. Only tonight.

"*Dušo*...sweetheart," he murmured against her neck, nuzzling aside her braid. She released a shaky breath before he kissed her again, his tongue stroking hers as they clung to each other.

Finally, she pulled back, and he nuzzled the freckle below her left ear, tracing his lips down the hollow at the base of her neck before nipping her collarbone above the neckline of her shirt. Sara nipped his earlobe, and he growled low. He couldn't get enough of her, couldn't wait to feel her bare skin against his.

"Hey," she said.

He kissed her again, lightly this time, letting his lips graze the soft skin at the edge of her mouth.

She slipped her hands under his shirt, and

each time her fingers grazed a new patch of skin, Gabe half whimpered, half roared. He took his time exploring each new inch of her exposed beneath the moonlight, loving the way she pressed against him, urging him onward. So responsive. So beautiful.

They stretched out on the blanket, and Sara wrapped her legs around his waist, straddling him, pressing her hips into his with the same hard urgency as her kisses.

Then he shifted and rolled her beneath him. She arched, and his breath quickened, overcome by how much he wanted her. By how much he needed her. He slid his hand beneath her shirt, then cupped her breast. He'd imagined this so many times, but the reality was so much better than any fantasy.

He pulled away and peeled off her shirt. His wasn't far behind. The rest of their clothes soon followed. The sight of her, naked on the grass, shining under the sky, made him harder than he could ever remember. He found himself mesmerized by the rise and fall of her chest until she rolled them, putting her on top and in charge, and Gabe found himself staring up at her. Her shoulders were cloaked in freckles, fading into the hollows of her collarbone, except for a single one atop her right breast. He wanted to become much better acquainted with that freckle.

"You are magnificent," she said, tracing her fingertips along his torso. "God, you're beautiful."

"You are," he answered, propping up on one elbow to kiss one pink nipple. A single curl had escaped her braid and now hung along her cheek, dangling near her jaw. Gabe twisted it around his finger, then brought it to his lips. "Take it down."

"What?"

"Your hair. Take it down. Let me see you in all your true glory." She started to protest, but he silenced her with a finger on her lips. "Please."

Slowly, eyes locked with his, Sara did as he asked. Until finally, all those gorgeous red curls spilled down around her shoulders and Gabe sank his hands into them, unable to help himself. She was like a Titian painting come to life. His very own Venus. He massaged her scalp, and Sara arched into his touch, amazing in her abandon. So sensitive to his touch. As if she were made just for him.

He took her all in, the pale skin shimmering in the moonlight, the gentle roundness of her breasts, the soft curve of her abdomen and the triangle of ginger curls below. He wanted to memorize it all even as he knew there'd never be enough time. They had tonight. Perhaps a couple weeks. But for now, she was here, with him, and he planned to savor her as much as possible.

Apparently, she felt the same, because she leaned forward then and began kissing a trail down his chest, over his thundering heart, past his abdomen, to his upper thighs. Her curls tickled his hard length, and he couldn't hold back a rough groan. Need clawed inside him, threatening to destroy him if he didn't have her soon. But then she took him into the warm wetness of her mouth, and he damned near embarrassed himself on the spot. All he could do then was close his eyes and slip his fingers into her silken hair, not to control her but to gently guide her to what felt best.

It was too much. It would never be enough. And all too soon, he was near the edge of orgasm.

Drawing on all his willpower, Gabe eased her away from him and pulled her up for a kiss, tasting himself on her lips. "Not yet, *dušo*. I want to taste you as well."

He eased her onto her back, then began trailing kisses down her luscious body, stopping at her breasts to pay homage, then continuing down to her softly rounded belly, before finally parting her thighs and taking in the scent of her arousal.

"Gabe, I need you…" She reached for him, but he wasn't budging. Not yet. Not until he'd claimed the treasure beneath that small triangle of auburn curls. Her hands dug into his hair, not pushing him away, but pulling him closer as he leaned in and dragged his tongue up the center of her slick folds.

"Oh, God," she moaned, arching into him, then holding him close as he made love to her with his lips and fingers, stroking her most sensitive flesh until she came apart in his arms, gasping and crying out his name to the heavens above.

His own need took charge then, and he slowly kissed his way up her body, reaching deftly for the strip of condoms he'd stashed beneath the corner of the blanket earlier and putting one on. Then he was stretched out above her, holding his weight on his forearms as he took in her dreamy, sated expression, her eyes cloudy with contentment and her small, satisfied smile notching his own desire higher.

"Are you ready for me, *dušo*?" he asked, his hard length poised at her wet entrance.

"Yes. So ready." Then she lifted her hips, and he thrust forward, sinking hilt deep into paradise.

They both held still a moment, drowning in sensation—so hot, so tight, so perfect. Then, slowly, carefully, Gabe began to move, setting a rhythm that had them both on the brink of climax all too soon.

Jaw tight, he reached between them with one hand to stroke her slick folds again. "Close, *dušo*?"

She whimpered and pushed her head back against the blanket, baring her neck to him, meeting him thrust for thrust. "Yes. Please, Gabe. I'm so close. Please…"

Then her body tightened around him, and she cried out her pleasure, spurring him closer to his own.

Gabe drove into her once, twice, then the tightly coiled energy at the base of his spine exploded into millions of iridescent shards of light, and he followed her into orgasm.

Reality returned in gentle waves. The rise and fall of her chest beneath his cheek. The sound of the birds and insects singing around them. The smell of plumeria and fresh growing things.

Sara's fingers traced tiny patterns against his scalp, and for that tiny, brief moment, there was no stress, no grief, no pain from the past, just the perfect bliss of a night in her arms. He closed his eyes and started to drift off, but her voice stopped him.

"What are you thinking about?" she asked quietly.

"I'm thinking about how wonderful you are, *dušo*," he said, kissing her stomach before moving off her to lie on the blanket at her side, then pulling her close again. "Why? What are you thinking?"

She shook her head, her curls spilling across his chest. "I'm glad you're here with me now."

"Hmm. Me, too." He kissed the top of her head and took a deep breath. It was true. There wasn't anywhere else he wanted to be right then. Normally, that would set off all the old wounds inside him, but tonight he felt none of them for some reason.

A beat passed, then Sara said, "I'm also thinking of Luke."

That got him raising his head to scowl down at her. "What?"

She shook her head. He wrapped his arms tighter around her and squeezed, his chest pinching with empathy as she sniffled. "What's wrong, *dušo*? Did I hurt you?"

"No. God, no. You've been wonderful." She pulled back, the moonlight glinting on her damp cheeks. "I'm honestly not sure what's happening with me right now. It's just being here with you tonight, and the whole trip, really, made me feel things I wasn't expecting. Made me feel like maybe there's more I could be doing with my life than just working in the PICU back in Chicago. These people down here, they really need you and what you do."

"As your tiny patients need you," Gabe said, kissing her forehead. "I'm sure they are very grateful for your help."

"Yes, but if I wasn't there, there're twelve other hospitals in the city that could serve their needs. Here, it's just you and the other volunteers at Hospital Los Cabreras. Without you, some of these people would die because they couldn't get care. I want to be needed, Gabe. I want to make a difference."

He took that in for a moment, settling her back against him and tracing his fingers up and down her spine as he stared up into the star-filled sky. Several beats passed before he answered, his own emotions swirling inside him in a jumbled mess—contentment, restlessness, exhaustion and something more, something deeper he wasn't ready to name yet. "Everyone can make a difference wherever they are. And just because you are needed somewhere does not mean you will save everyone. As a wise person once said, we must all do what we can, with what we have, where we are."

Sara sighed then kissed his chest, right over his heart. "You're right. I'm sorry."

"No need to be sorry." He held her closer still. "Things are what they are."

They lay quietly as fireflies flickered around them, and then he laughed, the deep sound echoing off the boulders nearby.

"What?" Sara asked, propping up on one elbow to look down at him. "What's so funny?"

"I'm just thinking that we finally have some privacy, and we spend it talking."

She smiled. "And what should we be doing?"

He growled and tugged her closer, nipping at her bottom lip. "This."

CHAPTER ELEVEN

THE NEXT FEW days went by in a blur for Sara. Between the busy clinics and the nights with Gabe—either sneaking away to their hilltop or catching quickies around the compound where they could—she felt like a teenager again.

She tried hard not to let it go to her head, though, reminding herself that this wasn't forever, just a fling. A very nice, very wonderful, very thought-provoking fling. But still a fling. In less than two weeks now, she'd be back in Chicago, working in her PICU, trying to get her son to call her between his busy class schedule and equally busy social life in California.

And Gabe would be here, continuing his work with the charity and moving on to someone else.

Something fierce and hot choked her insides, but she quickly shoved it away.

It wasn't jealousy, because she had nothing to be jealous of here. They'd both gone into this with their eyes open and their hearts closed.

Except, maybe, just maybe, hers had opened a bit to him without her consent.

Sara was sitting in her room in the dorms, just enjoying some quiet time tonight for a change. Doreen was out with Matteo, and Gabe had promised to help his friend Carlos fix some things on his property. Tristan had driven into San José for a meeting earlier that morning and wouldn't be back until the next day, so she'd decided to stay here and relax.

She'd just gotten into a new chapter in her book when a groan came from across the hall. Sara looked up at her open door and peered into Tristan and Noah's room. The light was on, and she could see shadows dancing across the wood floor. From where she sat, it appeared to be people rolling around on the bed. Ugh. Noah was her best friend and she loved Tristan, too, but that was one place in their lives that needed to remain private. She exhaled then shouted, "Close the door already!"

Tried to go back to her book, but pretty soon, another moan sounded, this one louder than before, followed by a very definite, "No!"

Noah's voice was rumpled and heavy, and the guy let out a half sigh, half whimper.

Crap.

Staring at the ceiling for a moment, Sara tried to decide what to do. Either things weren't going well between him and Tristan and she needed to intervene, or Noah was having a nightmare, in which case she probably shouldn't wake him.

But as the minutes crept by, the noises coming from Noah's room continued and grew louder, until she had to get up and find out what was going on in there. She set her book aside then padded across the hall on bare feet and stuck her head through the doorway. "Hey, can you keep it—"

The rest of that sentence died on her lips.

Noah was alone on his bed, his body rigid and his eyes rolled back in his head. Perspiration beaded on his forehead and upper lip, and his right cheek twitched.

Damn.

She'd seen this happen once before to him at the hospital in Chicago. They'd both been working a double shift, and he hadn't had time to eat or check his blood sugar properly. Sara rushed to his bedside and patted his cheek. "Noah? Noah, stay with me. It's Sara. Where are your glucose pills?"

He didn't respond.

Okay. Sugar. Need sugar. She dropped to her knees and dug for his bag under the bed, not caring where his clothes and books landed. *Where is it?* Finally, she located a cylinder of glucose tabs. Sara flipped open the lid to shake out an orange tablet, but it was empty.

Dammit.

Type I diabetics knew better than to let their supplies run out. Her blood ran cold despite the heat and humidity outside. She needed to find another source of sugar for him fast. Sara turned and began to rummage through the drawers of the dresser Matteo and Gabe shared, looking for anything that might work.

"What the hell's going on in here?" Gabe asked from the doorway.

She'd been in such a rush, she hadn't even heard him return.

"It's Noah," Sara said, cocking her head toward the bed. "He's hypoglycemic and needs sugar. His glucose tabs ran out."

Gabe cursed under his breath and ran a hand through his hair, mumbling something under his breath that Sara only half caught, something about having enough until the next order arrived. "Get in the drawer of my nightstand. There's some hard candy in there."

She did, pushing aside junk and a piece of paper with a name, Nisha, and a phone number scrawled on it. A tiny warning bell clanged in the back of her head, but she didn't have time to deal with it right then. Noah's life was on the line. She located a handful of brightly colored wrapped candies and pulled them out to hand to Gabe. "Here, stick one in his mouth."

He tried, but Noah knocked it away with a sneer.

Sara watched as the round candy rolled away under the bed, then nudged Gabe aside to roll Noah onto his side to shut off his insulin pump. Noah's eyes seemed to focus for half a second, then rolled back in his head again. "Hold his arms. You're stronger than I am. And I'll shove some candy in his mouth."

With a nod, Gabe did as she asked, securing Noah's arms an inch below the elbow. Noah continued to squirm and kick on the bed, his skin clammier by the second, but Gabe held tight.

"Be careful, he bites. And try break it up, it'll dissolve fast that way."

"I've got it." She grabbed another piece of candy and placed it atop the nightstand before smashing it with the big Bible sitting there. Then she turned back to Noah and forced his lips open, dropped the candy inside, then held his jaw shut for all she was worth, rubbing his throat with her free hand to make him swallow.

"What's going on up here?" Tristan said, skidding into the doorway. "I was on a conference call with the charity headquarters downstairs when I heard the ruckus. Oh, God." He rushed over to the bedside and dropped down on his knees, taking Noah's hand. "Baby, what's wrong?"

"His blood sugar dropped too low," Sara said. "He ran out of his glucose tabs, too. Why didn't he keep a backup?"

Tristan and Gabe exchanged a look.

Gabe sighed. "Our last shipment was short some medication, and we had villagers that are diabetic that needed the glucose tabs worse than Noah. We talked about it, and he promised me he had enough to last until our new shipment comes next week."

Sara stared at him a moment, trying not to be pissed and failing. "So, you told him it was okay?"

"No, I told him the situation, and he made the choice." Gabe's expression tightened. "Sometimes you have to make do with what you have here. That's what the candy is for."

"I see." Adrenaline still pulsed through her system, flaring hotter at his words. "I understand that choices have to be made, Gabe, but it shouldn't put one of your team members' lives at risk."

"Guys, can you fight about this later?" Tristan said, pushing the damp hair from Noah's forehead. "I think he needs more candy right now."

This time, Noah opened his mouth voluntarily, and Sara dropped the sugar inside.

Gabe let go of Noah's arms, then stepped back. Sara could feel him brooding near her back, but dammit, what happened tonight was wrong.

A minute or two ticked by in silence before Noah eased himself up onto an elbow.

"I turned your pump off," Sara said to

him, wiping her damp palms on her shorts. "Where's your meter?"

Noah pointed a shaky finger toward his bag on the floor. Gabe crouched to dig.

Sara nudged him out of the way again and grabbed the black-and-white case from the front pocket. "I saw it earlier."

"Thanks," Noah said, flopping back down on the bed, meter in hand.

While he and Tristan checked his blood sugar levels, Sara headed back across the hall to her own room, Gabe at her heels. He shut the door behind him, giving them some privacy.

"Look, I'm sorry about what happened tonight, but Noah's fine and—"

"He could've died," she said, voice tight. Heat prickled her cheeks, and to her horror, tears welled in her eyes. What was happening to her? She was not usually a crier. She would not cry. She was a trained nurse, for God's sake. But images of Noah convulsing on his bed, his skin cold and gray, kept filling her head. Soon, his face was replaced with her son, Luke's, and… Oh, God. She bit back a sob, and Gabe was there. Taking her into his arms and consoling her even though she was upset with him.

He rocked her gently, back and forth, his lips buried in her hair, whispering words in Croatian she didn't understand until, finally, her trembling subsided and her tears dried.

She pulled back a bit and swiped the back of her hand across her cheeks. "I'm sorry. I don't usually react like that. I'm not sure what's wrong with me at the moment."

"Noah is a friend," he said, cupping her cheeks and brushing away her remaining tears with the pads of his thumbs. "It's different when it's someone you know."

Sniffling, Sara pulled free from his arms and sat on the edge of her bed. "I can't understand why you'd let him go without his meds. Even with the candy."

Gabe sighed, hanging his head and rubbing the back of his neck. "He was not without his meds, Sara. He still had his insulin pump, and we've been monitoring him closely since his tabs ran out. He knew what to do if things went south, and he made the decision to forgo a refill this time so that others might receive help, too. It was all done with his consent. Life is hard here, Sara. I'm sorry this happened, but it all worked out in the end. If you want to be mad at someone, be mad at Noah for making the choice in the first place. People have a right to do what they want, Sara. Even if it goes against your wishes."

"Oh, I'm going to talk to him, all right," she said, flopping back to stare up at the ceiling. Excess energy still pinballed inside her, and she sat up again. "This isn't about my wishes. It's about safety."

He looked over at her a beat, then sank down beside her on the bed. "Noah is safe now. We're all here. Everything is fine. Be grateful for that. Not everyone is so lucky."

Crap.

She hadn't meant to bring up his painful past tonight, but it appeared that's exactly what she'd done. Sara took a deep breath then reached over for his hand. "Can you at least promise me that you and Noah won't make that choice again?"

"No." He kissed her hand, then gave her a sad smile. "But I can promise you that it will always be his choice. And I'll make sure he takes better care of himself so this doesn't occur again. Okay?"

It wasn't perfect, but it was better than nothing. Sara leaned in to rest her forehead against Gabe's. "Okay."

CHAPTER TWELVE

THE NEXT MORNING Sara shoved supplies into the bag at her feet. She'd agreed to help Gabe do his rounds in the village today, and he was already waiting at the exit for her. She was moving a bit slower than normal, what with tossing and turning most of the night following the drama with Noah, and then, when she had fallen asleep, having horrible dreams about Gabe and Noah and Luke all drowning and her having to choose only one to save. In the end, they'd all survived just fine, but she'd gone under because of her inability to make a decision.

There was a metaphor in there somewhere, she knew, but her tired, aching brain didn't want to think about it just then.

"Sorry," she said, handing him the bag. He shoved two mangoes inside the top, zipped it shut, then slung it over his shoulder. "Bit distracted, I guess. What's the fruit for?"

"You'll see. And I know the distracted feeling." He winked and held the tent flap for her, then followed her out. It was overcast today, and from the swelling, dark clouds on the horizon, rain would arrive soon. Gabe waited until they were outside the compound and on the road into the village before he took her hand. They'd both agreed to try to keep their affair discreet, although Doreen had seen them kissing with her own eyes, so it was doubtful the others didn't know that they were together.

Something cool and wet smacked the back of her neck as they reached the outskirts of the village, but Sara was so happy to be with Gabe, touching him again, that she didn't realize how bad the storm would be until the raindrops dumped from the sky all at once, soaking her to the core, and the ground beneath them turned to mud.

They ran toward the cover of trees.

Sara shook off the worst of the moisture from her hair, pulled on the plastic poncho from her bag, then smiled. "So, who's our first patient today?"

"Mrs. Godoy. She's one of my favorite patients here. I think you'll like her, too. One of the villagers who came in for an exam earlier said she'd developed an abscess. I'd like to check it out to make sure it's nothing." He finished tugging on his own poncho, then squinted out from their tree cover to point to a white house a few hundred feet away. It was raining so hard and fast it was nothing but a grayish blur against the sea of green to Sara. "Ready?"

"Ready." She barreled into the deluge, head down as mud kicked up behind her.

Gabe followed close on her heels, and they reached the front door at the same time. He knocked, then waited.

No answer.

Frowning, he tried again. "*Hola? Doña Godoy? Es el medico.* Dr. Novak," Gabe called.

"Is it locked?" Sara asked, trying the handle.

It wasn't. The door opened slightly, and through the slim crack, she could see an older woman sitting on a sofa against the wall in the living room. Sara would put her age at anywhere between sixty and eighty—it was hard to tell—and she looked incredibly thin and frail, as if she hadn't eaten in days, or maybe weeks.

Gabe leaned in behind Sara, then sighed. "She's worse than the last time I was here," he said, then raised a hand to the woman. "*Hola, Doña Godoy. Podemos entrar?*"

The woman stared at them a moment, then nodded. Gabe sidled around Sara, and she followed him inside, carrying the sharp scent of rain with them.

Sara peeled off her poncho as Gabe walked to the sofa and crouched, his smile easy. "*Cómo está?*"

Mrs. Godoy opened her mouth, then closed it, shrugging instead.

"She is one hundred and three years old," Gabe said, then asked the patient's permission before examining her arms for any signs of an abscess.

"Wow." Sara smiled and stepped forward beside Gabe. "That's impressive. Do you live here alone?"

Doña Godoy wheezed a faint, "*Sí...*"

Gabe nudged Sara's leg with his arm, then hiked his chin toward a lime-size lump on the woman's shoulder he'd revealed beneath the edge of her pastel-blue housedress. From the angry red lines streaking for the wound up toward the woman's neck and down toward her elbow, it was badly infected.

Gabe scowled as he pressed gently on the lump. "Her skin is feverish, at least a few degrees hotter than the air in here. *Duele?*"

Does this hurt?

The patient nodded, her gaze still locked on Sara, her expression stoic.

"*Que pasó?*" he asked Mrs. Godoy.

What happened?

Mrs. Godoy answered in a mix of broken Spanish phrases.

"This started as a bug bite," he translated. "She says it got infected, and someone from the village tried to treat her with camphor. It's a home remedy down here. They use it for everything, but this time it didn't work. Now she has this abscess. She needs antibiotics."

"Want me to set up an irrigation and drainage?" Sara reached for the supply bag near his feet.

"Yes. I'll need to numb the area first." He reached into the front pocket of the bag for a vial of lidocaine and a syringe as he explained the procedure to Mrs. Godoy in Spanish, then said to Sara, "Make sure you have plenty of gauze pads ready."

When he went to injection the medication, however, the patient jerked her arm away and scooted into the corner of the sofa. "No!"

Gabe put down the syringe and raised his hands. "*Todo es bueno, Doña Godoy. Todo es bueno.*"

The woman looked unconvinced, however, and shoved her hands beneath the sofa cushions while her entire body shook with the effort.

Sara knelt beside Gabe. "Maybe we can calm her down together, like we did Lalo." Then she smiled at the patient. "*Todo es bueno,*" she repeated.

It's all right.

"*Dr. Novak te ayudará.*"

Dr. Novak will help you.

"No!" Mrs. Godoy pulled her hands out from beneath the cushions to reveal a knife. Its wooden handle was gray with age and the serrated edge appeared dull from years of use, but that didn't stop the woman from brandishing it at them like a freshly sharpened machete.

Sara backed up, hands in the air, her pulse drumming in her ears. "Uh…what do we do now?"

Gabe never took his eyes off the patient, stone-cold calm as he whispered, "Don't move. I've got this."

He crept forward, keeping his hands where

Mrs. Godoy could see them. He'd left his scalpel and the syringe of medication out in the open and put himself between the patient and his supplies. In firm but quiet Spanish he said to the woman, "Look, I have nothing." He showed her his palms. "*Nada.*"

Mrs. Godoy lifted the knife an inch higher, and Sara's stomach plummeted to her toes.

"We're friends. You remember me, *sí?* Dr. Novak. I was here three months ago. You gave me two mangoes when I left. Look." He inched toward the supply bag and pulled out the two mangoes. Gabe set them on the sofa near Mrs. Godoy, the fruit's red and yellow skin stark against the beige upholstery. "I brought these for you."

The patient's gaze darted between the fruit and Gabe, then slowly, slowly, she lowered the knife to her lap. Sara released her pent-up breath as Gabe smiled and waggled his fingers at Mrs. Godoy.

"Give me your knife, and I'll peel one of these for you."

"*Marcharse,*" the woman mumbled. *Leave.*

Gabe's expression shifted from unreadable to desolate in under a second. This was a person he cared about, a patient he considered a friend, and she was turning down his aid.

Sara's heart broke for him, and she stepped forward, feeling like she had to do something to salvage the situation. "Hey, I can—"

Immediately, Mrs. Godoy raised the knife again, this time lurching forward, jabbing it in Sara's direction. "No! No!"

"Get back!" Gabe yelled, his gaze hot with anger as he scowled at Sara. "I told you not to move."

Shocked and hurt, she eased away again, and Mrs. Godoy lowered the knife.

"Your arm is infected. I want to help you," Gabe said in Spanish to his patient after a final warning glare at Sara. He picked up a mango then pointed at the sofa. "May I sit?"

Mrs. Godoy blinked at him a moment, considering his request, then nodded. Gabe eased down onto the sofa, careful to move slowly. The mango still sitting there rolled into his side as he held the other one in his hand up to his nose. Then he pointed at the knife again. "*Por favor?*"

Finally, the handed it to him as tears rolled down her cheeks.

Sara's heart broke anew.

"*Gracias.*" Gabe peeled the mango, then offered Mrs. Godoy a slice. She took it with trembling fingers.

"I am tired," she said around a bite of mango. "I do not want this."

Gabe stared down at the mango rinds in his lap, and Sara knew he had to be thinking about his family back in Croatia. How he'd failed to save them then. How it must feel similar to him now, with his patient refusing care. She wanted to go to him, hold him, tell him none of this was his fault, but she didn't dare move from her spot again and risk his anger.

"If you don't let me help you, you'll get very sick," he said, wiping his hand on his scrub pants, keeping his tone carefully neutral. "I may not be here to help you. You could die."

The patient gave a tiny shrug, then took another bite of mango.

Gabe hung his head, and that's when Sara knew it was over.

It felt as if all the energy left her body, and Sara sank down to sit on the floor, tucking her legs beneath her.

After a little while longer, Gabe started peeling the mango again, scowling and speaking to no one in particular. "I can give her antibiotics, but I don't think that will be enough." He offered Mrs. Godoy another slice of mango. "I doubt she'll even take them at this point."

Sara opened her mouth, then closed it again. They'd talk about this later, she was sure, but for now there wasn't anything left to say.

So, they sat together in silence, listening to the rain and sharing slices of mango. Every so often, Gabe would ask Mrs. Godoy if she was sure. If letting nature take its course was what she really wanted. If she really understood what that choice meant. Each time, his tone grew more pained and desperate. And every time Mrs. Godoy chose to die, Sara wept inside for them both.

CHAPTER THIRTEEN

GABE HAD BEEN awake since well before dawn, unable to stop thinking about Doña Godoy and how he'd been forced to leave her alone in that house to die. Short of restraining the old woman and forcibly performing surgery on her wound, there wasn't much he could do, but still. Each hour that ticked by tightened like a noose around his neck.

He got up and fumbled around in the dark for his things, then headed out of the dorms to the showers and latrine. Sara had been concerned about him, but all he'd wanted last night was to be left alone with his thoughts. His failures.

The last thing he wanted to do was burden her with those. Not when they had precious little time left together. Besides, he wouldn't have been good company. He got ready then headed to the clinic tent, not hungry at all and wanting to get on with the day so he could stop thinking about Doña Godoy every second and how it reminded him of those last hours in the ruins of the apartment in Vukovar.

Hours. Hours had gone by that day, in a blur of terror and torment and unspeakable loss. Marija had seemed alright, focused solely on saving their son, starting the CPR on Karlo before he'd arrived and helping him with it afterward. But the longer they'd worked on Karlo, the paler she'd become, her movements growing weaker until she'd collapsed, and he'd discovered the wound in Marija's side was worse than she'd let on. She'd been slowly bleeding out internally. By then, with no access to the medical supplies and equipment he'd needed, there was nothing to be done. Looking back now, if he'd left Karlo for dead, there would have been a chance he could've saved Marija, but how could he have made that choice? He couldn't. And in the end, he'd lost them both.

Volunteers slowly filed into the tent as clinic opening drew near. Gabe kept to his exam area in the back, fiddling with his supplies and trying to look busy so no one would talk to him. It worked pretty well, too, at least until Sara showed up.

"Hey." She walked into his area and pulled the curtain to give them a modicum of privacy. "How are you? Yesterday was tough, I know."

"I'm fine," he bit out, turning away from her instead of pulling her close like he wanted. He craved her comfort and support, but that wasn't what they'd agreed to. They'd agreed to a fling. Nothing more. No strings attached. And Gabe felt like nothing but strings today. So he pushed her away, emotionally. "You should get your station ready. There's a line of patients outside already. Busy day."

For a moment, it looked like she wanted to argue with him, but thankfully, she let it drop. "Okay. I'll see you later, then."

He grunted, not trusting himself not to beg her to come back, then nodded to the volunteer near the door to let the first patients in.

From there, the day passed fairly quickly, with Noah assisting Gabe with numerous lacerations, several blood pressure checks, a couple of broken bones to set and one teenager with what he suspected was fairly severe appendicitis that required surgery and lavage.

By the time he was done, Gabe was exhausted. Unfortunately, he was no less distracted from his troubles, though. They hung over him like a thundercloud, ready to bluster away all the happiness he'd managed to build the last couple of weeks with Sara. Just like always. Ruined again.

"Everything okay, Doc?" Noah asked as he helped clean up the exam area after their last patient.

"Fine," Gabe said, more out of habit than anything. He wasn't a talker when it came to his problems. Never had been. Marija used to get so angry with him about that. And damn if that reminder didn't make his chest ache even more than it already did.

"Huh." Noah stuffed a trash bag full of crumpled paper and packaging. "Because between you and Sara, I'm not sure who looks more depressed."

He scowled over at her station, only to find her gone already. Just as well, since all he wanted to do tonight was get drunk at the bar in the village and forget. "Everything's fine, okay? Forget it."

Noah snorted. "Okay, sure. No problem. Consider it forgotten."

Except knowing the guy as well as Gabe did, the subject wouldn't get dropped at all.

He loved Noah, but the guy was worse than a woman when it came to talking things to death.

Gabe hurried up and finished putting everything away in the exam area, then hurried from the tent, barely stopping at his dorm room to change clothes before heading out of the compound and into the village alone. It wasn't until the gates closed behind him that he felt like he could breathe again, or at least breathe better. Because it still felt like there was a ten-ton weight of guilt pressing the oxygen from his lungs. That never went away, not really. Sometimes it lightened, like when he'd been with Sara. But it was always there, always waiting to return to steal his joy.

Instead of Alma's, he headed to another small bar on the opposite side of the village called Rosa's and grabbed a stool, ordering tamales and a beer.

"*Hola,*" a female voice said, and he looked up to see Nisha, the cashier from the market, smiling at him. "I haven't seen you in Rosa's before, Doc."

He took a sip from his bottle, then smiled at her over the top. "First time. What are you doing here?"

"I work here part-time," she said in Spanish. "When I'm not at the market."

She was too young for him by a good decade or more, and Gabe wasn't really interested in her that way anyway, but she was bright and bubbly, and she made a nice distraction when he really needed one most. So he gestured toward the stool beside his. "Please, sit."

The woman laughed. "Can't. I'm working tonight. But I'll stop by on my break and we can chat, Doc."

There was a satellite TV on the wall behind the bar, and he lost himself in the soccer game and his beer until his food arrived. A haze of cigarette smoke hovered near the ceiling, and the air smelled of booze and bad decisions, but it fit his mood perfectly. He'd just finished his last tamale and fourth beer when the young woman sat down on the stool beside him again.

He had a nice little buzz going when she reached over and brushed the hair off his forehead with her fingers. It sent a tiny shiver through him and made her smile. She had a dimple on the right side. He'd never noticed that before.

"You're very handsome, Doc," she said,

bending forward slightly to give him a peek down her shirt. "Even if you're drunk."

Gabe snorted and finished off his latest beer in one long swig. "I'm not drunk. And you're cute."

"Am I?" She placed a hand on each of his thighs and leaned into the vee between his legs. That would've been a great time to put a stop to the nonsense, but there was someone behind him and he had nowhere to go, so he stayed, holding up a hand to stop her. Unfortunately, that hand landed on her chest instead.

"Oops," he said, pulling away fast.

"Oops is right," another female voice said to his right, sharp enough to cut glass. "What the hell are you doing here? I've been looking for you for hours, Gabe. I was worried."

Sara.

The younger woman sat back fast and excused herself, and Gabe knew he'd messed up big-time, but his alcohol-muddled mind was still working out why. "I'm fine," he said, tossing his credit card on the bar and wobbling slightly on his stool. "No need to worry."

"Yes," she said, crossing her arms and narrowing her gaze. "I can see you're just peachy keen."

"Peachy keen?" Gabe scrunched his nose. "Who says that anymore?"

She glared daggers at him. "Are you ready to leave?"

"If you want." He shrugged.

"Yes, I want, Gabe."

"Fine." He stood and took a second to get his bearings. Good thing he'd had those tamales, because the beer was hitting him hard tonight for some reason. "Why are you mad?"

"I'm not mad," she said, though the edge in her voice proclaimed the exact opposite. They headed outside into the dark, cool night. "Can you walk back to the compound?"

"Of course." He scoffed. "I'm not—"

"Gabe," the woman called from the entrance. "You forgot your credit card."

"Oh." He turned back, the weight of Sara's look burning a hole through his spine. "Thanks."

"The last two were on the house," she said in Spanish.

"No." Gabe waved her off. "How much?"

"Our treat." She gave him that flirty little smile again, the one that made him feel ancient and all kinds of wrong. "We want to make sure you'll come back."

He took a deep breath and pulled out his wallet from the back pocket of his jeans. Put the credit card in then pulled out an American twenty-dollar bill instead and handed it to her. The last thing he wanted was to feel indebted to her. "Here then. For you."

Her dimple showed again as she grinned. "*Gracias*, Doc. *Buenas noches.*"

"*Buenas noches, señorita,*" he mumbled, turning back to Sara, who waited where he'd left her.

"Nice seeing you again," Sara called to her over his shoulder, her tone dripping with angry sarcasm. That's when he knew this wasn't going to end well at all.

Gabe took Sara by the arm and steered her back toward the compound. "Will you stop being rude?"

She shook free of him. "Will you stop being so friendly?"

"Well, I'm glad one of us is tonight." The minute the words were out, he regretted them, but all of his filters seemed to be gone. Along with the nice distracting buzz he'd had going on in the bar. Now that the cool breeze was slapping him on the cheeks, it was reawakening all his old pain.

The guilt. The sorrow. The failure.

Sara charged ahead down the road, not waiting for him. "What were you doing in there, anyway?"

"Trying to have fun," he said, catching up to her. He felt bad enough as it was—he didn't need her piling on to his pain. Defensive anger bubbled up inside him. "Is that a crime now?"

"No." She gave a dismissive wave, not even looking at him. "If it's fun you want, go have it. I can go back to the compound by myself."

"Why are you making such a big deal out of this, Sara?" he said, making some nearby chickens squawk in their coop. *Shit.* He lowered his voice a tad. "I don't need a keeper. I'm not a child."

"Then stop acting like one and talk to me. I know you're upset about what happened with Mrs. Godoy yesterday. I was there, remember. But instead, you run off to the bar and her."

"I did not run to that woman," he growled. This was getting ridiculous. "I needed a drink, to take my mind off things and she happened to be there. How was I supposed to know she works in that bar?"

Sara snorted. "I don't know, Gabe. Maybe because you have her phone number in your nightstand?"

"What the hell are you talking about?" They'd left the village behind, and the streetlights here were few and far between. Shadows slanted long across both of them, which only made it worse. He wanted to see her face, read her emotions, but all he had to go by here were her words. And what she'd told him in the past. "Wait a minute. Okay, yes. Fine. She gave me her number once, months ago. I shoved it in the drawer and figured I'd throw it out later. I forgot."

"Uh-huh. Sure." She crossed her arms, gaze narrowed. "I asked you to do one thing for me, Gabe, when we started this fling. Don't lie."

"I'm not lying."

"No. You just let some woman come on to you in a bar while we're sleeping together."

To hear her talk so casually about their connection when it meant so much to him cut Gabe to the bone. Between the alcohol in his system and the ache in his heart, he lashed out angrily. "I am not your ex-husband, Sara. If you have baggage from him, don't dump it on me."

"Excuse me?" She all but spat the words, then started off down the road again. "This has nothing to do with that."

"Really?" He stalked after her, getting more pissed off by the step. "Because it seems like it does."

"Well, you're wrong."

He gave a harsh chuckle. "Yeah? Is that why you keep walking away from me?"

"No." She stopped and rounded on him. "What do you want from me, Gabe?"

Everything.

That caught him up short. No. He couldn't want everything with Sara, because everything was impossible. He wanted to go back thirty years and never leave his apartment in Vukovar. He wanted to start this whole mission trip over again just to relive the past weeks with Sara. He wanted to stop himself from going to that damned bar tonight. But since none of those options were viable, he said the one that was. "I want to go back to the compound."

He walked around her and headed home, all too aware of the irony of him walking away this time.

Her laugh cut through the darkness like a scalpel, halting him in his tracks. "There you go again. Shutting out everyone. Shutting out the world. Do you ever let anyone in, Gabe?"

"Not anymore," he called back. "Been there. Done that. Have the scars to prove it."

This time it was Sara who ran up to him, her footsteps echoing loud through the darkness. "So, that's it then?"

"Yep. I guess it is." He felt all kinds of wrong inside, like he was making a huge mistake but was completely incapable of stopping it. Honestly, now that he looked back on these last couple of weeks, it was inevitable, really. That things would end as abruptly as they'd started. This was exactly why he didn't do relationships anymore. They never worked out. She wanted too much from him. Wanted things he couldn't give. Things he just didn't have anymore. Things that had died that day in Vukovar with his family.

Things like forever. Things like his heart.

"I'm sorry," he said as they reached the compound gates. "I never led you on. I told you up front what this was between us. A fling, nothing more. I'm not capable of more, Sara."

Under the orangish glow of the streetlight, she stared at him, her copper eyes ablaze with hurt. Then she lowered her head, and he wished he'd been better, done better, but he couldn't. When she looked up at him again, her smile was anything but pleasant. "You're right. We set the rules from the start, and I should obey them now. I just wanted to help you, Gabe."

"I don't want your help." *Liar.* He wanted it more than his next breath, but he was too far gone to stop now, so he kept on going. "I don't want to be pitied or saved, Sara. I just want to be left alone."

She flinched, like he'd physically hurt her, but then her professional mask fell back into place and she nodded, stepping back from him, giving him space.

"Right. Okay." Her icy expression should've frozen the rain forest. "Your wish is granted."

Then Sara walked away, leaving Gabe behind to watch her go.

Same as always.

CHAPTER FOURTEEN

GABE WOKE TO a heinous, earsplitting sound, certain the world was ending. But no. That had happened the night before. Cursing under his breath, he pulled a pillow over his face to drown out the horror of all his mistakes and failures, but they just kept coming. At least it was not a clinic day, so he didn't have to try to be cordial to people, because right then it felt like his head might actually explode.

Finally, he sat up, scowling, to find Noah looking far too chipper for his own good after what he'd been through a few nights before and singing loud enough to wake everyone in Costa Rica. Maybe everyone in Nicaragua and Panama, too.

"What the—?" He squinted into the too-bright room. "What time is it?"

"Almost ten," Noah said, whistling as he carried this towel and toiletries out the door, thankfully taking that god-awful song with him. Gabe flopped back down again, his eyes closing before his head hit the pillow. After drinking so much and sleeping so little, death might honestly be a better alternative this morning. Or at least a coma. Anything, really, that would allow him to forget last night and his fight with Sara.

Oh, God. Sara.

He ground the heels of his hands against his scratchy eyes then winced. Once she'd walked away from him, he'd wandered around the compound, checking supplies and doing stupid busywork until sunrise, then he'd stumbled in here and collapsed on his bed with all his clothes on, eyes burning from exhaustion.

There you go again. Shutting out everyone. Shutting out the world. Do you ever let anyone in?

Those words kept looping through his head, flaying him open anew with each pass.

Truth was, no, he didn't let people in. Because letting them in meant being vulnerable.

And he was through with vulnerable.

Vulnerable brought you nothing but hurt and pain and despair.

Vulnerable cost you everything, and he had

nothing left to give. Life had taken it all away from him.

Even Sara.

He groaned and rolled over, burying his face in the mattress and drifting off into blissful nothingness again.

The next time his eyes fluttered open, it was because of his stomach growling. The sweet, yeasty smell of fresh-baked bread filled his nose, and he licked his dry lips, croaking, "What time is it?"

"Almost two in the afternoon," Noah said from his bed, looking at Gabe from over the top of a book. "I brought you some toast and a glass of water from the kitchens."

"Hmm." Gabe sat up once more and scratched his head, yawning and squinting around. His head wasn't pounding so much anymore, but his heart still ached like mad. He took a deep breath and swung his legs over the bed, frowning down at his mud-speckled shoes. "Dammit. I haven't slept in my clothes since college."

"Not a good look on you, bro," Noah said, not looking at him this time. "Want to talk about it?"

"No." Definitely not. He and Noah were friends, but the guy was Sara's bestie. That

would not go well for Gabe. He got to his un-
steady feet, then started toward the hall. "I'm
going to shower."

"Might want to take a towel with you. And
soap. And clothes," Noah called from behind
him, stopping him short.

Grumbling, Gabe turned to head back into
the room, only to find his world went topsy-
turvy. He gripped the door frame like a lifeline and closed his eyes against a wave of
sudden nausea.

"Yeah." Noah wrapped an arm around his
waist and helped him back to the bed. "Sit
down and talk to me." He went back to sit on
his own bed across from Gabe. "Seriously.
We're the only ones up here, and I won't say a
word to Sara, if that's what you're concerned
about."

Gabe wanted to tell him no, but shaking his
head was a precarious thing at the moment,
so he just grunted instead.

"Look," Noah said. "I know you two are
going through something right now. Sara
looked like death warmed over at breakfast,
too, so…"

That knowledge did little to make Gabe
feel better, since it was his fault.

"Anyway. Talk to me. It helps, I promise.

You care for her—I know you do. I can see it every time you look at her."

Gabe opened his mouth to deny it, but what was the point? He was too tired to argue anyway. "It's over."

"What?" Noah frowned. "The thing between you and Sara?" At Gabe's look, he grinned. "Everyone's known for a while now you guys were an item."

"Not an item." Gabe reached for the glass of water and took a long gulp to quench his parched throat. Not ready to risk the toast yet, though. "Just a fling."

"Hmm." Noah did not look convinced. "Really? Because the way you two were flitting around here like a couple of Disney characters in love, it looked like more to the rest of us."

"I do not flit." He scowled.

Noah laughed. "Maybe not, but there was still some definite magic happening there."

He took a deep breath and tried to get up again, but his legs weren't having it. Man, he really needed to not drink anymore. He wanted to be gone from there. Wanted to escape the spotlight and lick his wounds in private. Wanted to bury his head under a rock and not come out again for years, maybe ever.

But Noah was having none of it. "Sara needs someone to care for her," he said quietly after a beat or two. "She deserves that. Deserves a partner who will be there for her, who can be strong so she doesn't have to be all the time. Who'll tell her the truth, even if it hurts."

Gabe cringed. "That's not me."

"It could be." Noah met his gaze and held. "Or I thought so, anyway. Look, man. We've worked on these missions together for a while now, and I know you've got a lot of bad stuff in your past, Gabe. But you're still here. You survived. You kept going. That means something."

"I shouldn't have." He hung his head, bile and bitterness burning his throat. "I'd give anything to not be here if it meant my wife and child survived."

Silence grew taut between them, until Noah said, "You know, when I first realized I was gay, I thought my world was over. I would've given anything to be straight. But we can't change who we are, and we can't control what happens to us. All we can do is keep surviving. Keep going until it gets better. Because it always does if we hang in there long enough."

"God." Gabe threw back his head, decades of pain bursting past his long-held walls now. "Do not even try to come in here with that inspirational crap with me. I watched my son and my wife die in my arms. It was my fault. If I hadn't been so stubborn, so determined to do what I wanted, they wouldn't have been there. I live with that guilt and grief every single day. There is no surviving or better here. There is just penance. That's all I deserve."

"What a load of crap."

The shock of those words had Gabe blinking at Noah, stunned. "I'm sorry?"

"I said, what a load of crap." Noah shook his head, giving Gabe a look. "I'm not saying what happened to you wasn't awful, because it sounds like it was. But do you honestly think this is what they'd want for you? Your wife and you son? To wallow in sadness and self-pity and squander the precious life you still have?"

Gabe opened his mouth, closed it, then opened it again, speechless.

"Because I'd think they'd want you to be happy. Mourn them. Put them to rest. Then move on." Noah stood and paced their small room. "God, Gabe. You have so much to offer. You're such a good man. Dedicated.

Hardworking. Loyal. Kind. Don't waste all that on a memory. Use what time you have left to be happy. To live a life that you love. And if that's with Sara, great. If it's not, that's okay, too. But don't dishonor the lives and memories of your family by throwing away what you've got. Don't let the worst day of your life steal the best ones."

He sagged back against the wall, letting it all sink in. He'd never thought about it like that. In all the years since Marija and Karlo had died, he'd carried that weight with him because it was easier and safer than putting it down and trying to live again. But now...

Sara's face flashed in his head. Her smiles during the clinic. The sunlight in her hair that day at Carlos's house. The feel of her beneath him, around him, when they made love on their hilltop.

This thing between them might have started out as a fling, but Gabe realized now that it had become so much more. It was his lifeline. His heart and soul. His everything.

He glanced across the hall, but her room was empty.

Right.

Well, he owed her an apology, if nothing else. An explanation about last night and a promise to do better in the future, if she'd listen and have him.

He wasn't sure yet about where the days ahead would take him or even if she'd want to be in a real relationship with a man like him, but he was determined to find out.

Gabe stood and headed for the door again, steadier now, a man with a mission.

"Where are you going?" Noah asked from behind him.

"To find Sara."

"Might want to clean up first, dude. You look like hell," Noah said, snorting. "And eat your damned toast, too."

After shoving a triangle of buttery bread into his mouth, Gabe grabbed his towel and toiletries and headed for the hall, ready to clean up his life—in more ways than one.

"Hey," Doreen said, taking a seat beside Sara on her bench near the front of the compound. "Everything okay?"

Sara shrugged and tried to continue reading, but it was hard when it felt like the life she'd planned was collapsing down around her. She'd come here to Costa Rica looking for direction, for purpose, and she'd be leaving with a broken heart.

Typical.

Not to mention she'd slept badly last night again, replaying that fight with Gabe and all the horrible things they'd said to each other like a never-ending movie in her mind.

I don't want your help. I don't want to be pitied or saved, Sara. I just want to be left alone.

Well, that was her told, wasn't it? She sighed. God, why couldn't she just leave it? Why did she always have to try to control everything? Maybe her ex was right. That's the excuse he'd given her, anyway, for why he'd screwed around. For freedom, to break the ties she'd bound around him.

Bastard.

She scowled down at her book. Why was trying to take care of people so wrong? She had the best intentions at heart. Why couldn't others see that? She just wanted to help them.

I don't want your help.

Gabe's voice rang through her head like a clarion call.

"Did I ever tell you about my husband?" Doreen asked, breaking into Sara's dreadful thoughts. "My Martin."

Sara gave the woman some side-eye. "I didn't know you were married."

"I'm not anymore." Doreen gave a sad smile. "He passed away last year. That's why I'm on hiatus from the show."

"Oh. I'm so sorry." Now Sara felt even worse. She'd been so wrapped up with Gabe she hadn't even gotten to know her roommate beyond the superficial. "That's terrible."

Doreen nodded. "We were married thirty years. He was my first love. We met in high school."

"Wow. That's a long time."

"Yes, it is." Doreen sat back, glancing up at the darkening sky as thunder rumbled in the distance. "We did everything together. Were best friends. He was a cardiologist. We traveled the world, made a home and family together. I thought it would last forever."

Unable to stop herself, Sara reached over to take Doreen's hand. "What happened?"

"Cancer." She shrugged, blinking hard. "Still makes me tear up, thinking about it. By the time they discovered it, it had already metastasized to his brain and bones. Stage four. We tried a couple rounds of chemo and radiation but then called it quits. It wasn't going to change the outcome, so why ruin the quality of the life he had left?"

Sara didn't know what to say, so she just stayed quiet, offering silent support for a friend in need.

"That's why I came here," Doreen said at last.

"To the mission trip?"

"No. To Costa Rica. This was supposed to be our last trip together. Martin wanted to see the rain forests and the nature. After he passed, it felt like my duty to come down here and see it for him. But sitting on my butt at some fancy resort didn't feel right, so I volunteered with the charity. Took some time off from filming the TV show, and here I am."

Sara's heart broke all over again for Doreen. "That's really brave of you."

"Hmm." Doreen looked over at her. "I'm not the only brave one, though. Look at you, risking your heart with Gabe."

"Oh. No." She shook her head. "It wasn't like that."

"You mean you two weren't involved? Because it certainly looked that way to the rest of us."

Heat prickled Sara's cheeks. "No. I mean, we were involved. But it was just a fling. And it's over now anyway, so it doesn't matter."

Doreen watched her a moment, then nodded and looked off toward the pitch-black clouds and lightning on the horizon. They'd have to go in soon or risk another deluge, from the looks of it. "That's too bad. You two seemed perfect for each other."

"I thought so, too," Sara said, then bit her lips. Whoops. Hadn't mean to say that out loud. But it was true, no matter how much she'd like to deny it. Even going into it all with her eyes open and her heart closed hadn't helped. She'd opened up and fallen for Gabe hard. Which only made losing him even worse. She'd thought maybe, finally, after all this time, she'd finally found the one. Her person. But apparently not. "He lied to me."

"Yeah?" Doreen raised a brow. "That sucks. About what?"

"The cashier at the store in town. He said they were just friends, but he had her phone number in his nightstand, and when I found him in a bar in the village last night, she was all over him."

"Wow." Doreen looked stunned. "That doesn't sound like Gabe at all. I mean, I don't really know him that well, but that's pretty cold. You were married before, right?"

"Yep." The first raindrops splattered on her bare legs, and Sara tucked them under her. The large tree above them would keep them dry, but this probably wasn't the best spot to be with the lightning. The sky above had taken on a weird greenish-charcoal color, making the vegetation stand out almost white against the ominous clouds. "He lied to me, too. Used to sleep around. That's how I recognize the signs."

"Hmm." Doreen nodded, still staring at the horizon. "Yeah, I can see how that would look through your lens."

"My lens?"

"Sure. We all have them. The things we filter our experiences through. What make us who we are." Doreen smiled at her. "It's not a bad thing, as long as we're aware of them. Take me, for instance. I filter everything through the lens of my marriage to Martin now. Our time together and how he treated me. If a man can't live up to that, then byebye."

Sara took that in for a moment, Gabe's words from the night before ringing again in her head.

I am not your ex-husband, Sara. If you have baggage from him, don't dump it on me.

Was that what she'd been doing last night? Putting her past issues on her present problems?

"Anyway, I'm not saying that Matteo and I are going to tie the knot or anything," Doreen continued. "But he's the real deal. A good man. Beneath his tough exterior. I thought maybe Gabe was, too." She shifted slightly to face Sara. "Did you ask him what happened at the bar?"

"Yes." *No.* She'd been so upset and worried last night that by the time she'd arrived at the bar, she'd been on pins and needles. And honestly, she'd taken her stress and frustration about it out on him. Damn. She'd seen that Nisha woman with her hands on him, and it had made Sara realize that she wanted more with Gabe. She wanted him to be hers. Exclusively. Forever. And that went against all their rules and agreements and had only made her more frustrated and upset and rubbish.

She hung her head and sighed. "I messed up. I called it off. It's my fault it's over."

"Can you talk to him now about it?" Doreen asked as the rain started to fall steadier. It was dark enough now that the streetlights had clicked on even though it was still afternoon. "Looks like we're in for a heck of a storm."

"Yep. We should probably head back to the dorms," Sara said, deftly avoiding the last question for now.

They stood and began to hurry back down the road when shouting came from the gate behind them.

"Help! Please help me. *Por favor!*"

Sara turned to find Carlos standing there, his tanned face pale with fear. She rushed over to him. "What's wrong? What's happened?"

"It's Esme," he said. "She was with me in the yard, playing with the chickens and gathering eggs in the coop. I only looked away for a second, but she was gone. Then I heard her screaming and…" He lapsed into Spanish then, rushed and broken, and Sara could only get every third or fourth word, which she tried to piece together as best she could.

"Wait. Wait. She fell into a hole?" Sara said, holding up a hand to calm the man. "Take a breath."

"*Cavernas…*" Carlos said after a moment and a deep inhale. "Down by the river. I've told Esme not to play there many times. She doesn't listen. I keep an eye on her, but tonight

I turned my back for one second and she disappeared. She goes into the caves and tunnels to play sometimes." His voice caught, and he cleared his throat. "Please come. Hurry! The *cavernas* flood during the storms and she'll be drowned!"

Cavernas. Caves. *Oh, God.*

Thinking on her feet was Sara's bread and butter, and she was in her element now. She turned and called back to Doreen, letting her know what was happening. "Find Gabe and get the others. I'm going with Carlos now to make sure Esme's okay. Tell them to hurry!"

Then she was through the gate and running down the road toward the village, wind slapping her face and the first fat raindrops splattering the ground, praying like hell they weren't too late.

CHAPTER FIFTEEN

GABE HAD JUST finished dressing after his shower when Doreen came barreling down the hall of the dorms. "Hurry! Sara needs help!"

His blood froze, and his chest constricted. He rushed to the door of his room, Noah close behind. "What's happened?"

"Carlos, your friend from the village, came to the gates and said his daughter is lost in the caves down by the river. She goes in there sometimes to play." She paused for a breath. "He said they flood during the storms and if he can't get her out, she'll drown. Sara went with him to make sure the little girl is okay, but she'll need backup."

Dammit.

He immediately switched to emergency mode, shouting orders and preparing for the worst, even as he prayed inside that everyone would be okay. It was like a switch was flipped, shutting off his emotions, because if he dwelled on the fact that this felt very much like history repeating itself, he'd end up in a corner somewhere bashing his head against a wall.

They would be okay. They had to be okay.

Because if anything happened to Esme, he'd never forgive himself.

And if anything happened to Sara, he couldn't survive. Not again.

"Noah, grab the supply kits from the clinic tent and round up as many volunteers as you can to help. Doreen, find Matteo and get into the maintenance building. We'll need rope and flashlights and anything else you think might be helpful in an outdoor rescue situation that you can carry easily." He jammed his feet into his boots then headed out the door. "I'm going to make sure a crowbar and jack are ready in the truck in case we need to move or lift anything heavy. Those caves are known to have lots of rock collapses and debris in them. Meet me at the gates in five minutes and we'll head over together. Wear your ponchos. It's nasty out there."

People scattered, and Gabe tugged on his rain gear then headed down to start the truck.

Then he checked in the bed for the items he needed and added a huge stack of blankets, just in case. If poor little Esme had been in the water a long time, she'd need warming up. The temperatures might be in the seventies and eighties here, but the torrents pouring down from the hilltops were much colder. Hypothermia could set in within minutes, especially if a person was injured and in shock already.

He drove down to the gates, the wheels spinning slightly on the muddy roadway, then waited for what felt like forever until the rest of them showed up. Rain was coming down in sheets now, making it nearly impossible to see more than a few feet into the distance. Based on the thick clouds above obscuring the light, it could've been four in the morning instead of four in afternoon.

They piled their gear into the bed of the truck, along with Doreen and Matteo and four other volunteers, while Noah climbed into the passenger seat with him. Gabe barely waited for him to shut the door before he took off.

"I told Tristan what was happening," Noah said, clutching the door with one hand to steady himself as they bounced over ruts in the road. In his other hand he held the satellite phone from the office. "He gave me this, in case we need to call for more assistance."

Gabe shook his head. "The nearest level-one trauma center is in San José. Two hours away. If Esme needs more assistance than we can provide, she'll die."

God, please don't let her die.

Even with the driving rain and the mud and the darkness, he managed to arrive at Carlos's property on the far side of the village in record time. Gabe pulled up as close to the forest at the back of the property as possible, alarming the chickens in the process, then slammed the transmission into Park and got out, leaving the truck running with the headlights on for illumination.

Carlos was standing near the tree line, looking despondent and wringing his hands. Gabe ran over to his friend and took him by the shoulders. "What happened? Where's Sara?"

"Esme was playing here by the chicken coop and I was making dinner. I had to go inside to check on the food and told her to stay where she was, but when I came back out, she was gone." He was a big man, brawny and strong from working outside, but Carlos was shaking like a leaf now.

"Then I heard her screaming and ran down to the riverbank. She said she was lost in the caves. I could hear her but couldn't see her. It's so dark in there, and the water was already up to my ankles. I knew I had to get her out and I needed help, so I ran to the compound to find you. Sara was at the gate and said she'd get word to you. Then she came with me. I told her not to go down there alone, to wait for you, but she wouldn't listen. Why won't they listen to me?"

Gabe's gut dropped into a black hole of dread. "Sara's down there now, by the river, in the caves with Esme?"

His friend nodded. "I'm sorry, Gabe. I told her not to go without you, but she said she couldn't wait."

For a moment, the pounding of the rain and rushing of the river nearby transformed into bombs and bullets in his head, and the rain forest blurred to the crumbling wreckage of his apartment building back in Vukovar. The air was thick with the acrid stench of gunpowder and dust, choking out everything except the rush of adrenaline and anguish inside him.

"Gabe!" Noah called, jarring him back to the present. "What should we do first?"

He took a deep, steadying breath and focused on the here, the now, the danger little Esme and the woman he loved were in. He'd save them. Save them both. Or die trying.

"Right. Set up a triage unit here. I'm going to go down to the riverbank and see what's happening there. Hand me one of the flashlights from the back of the truck, please." While he waited for that, he grasped Carlos's shoulders tighter, forcing the scared man to look at him. "I'll get them back. I promise."

Carlos nodded and Noah handed him a flashlight, then Gabe was off, dodging trees as he headed into the rain-dark night. Water pelted his face and body, but he didn't care. All he cared about now was finding Esme and Sara and keeping them safe. Nothing else mattered.

The closer he got to the river, the louder the rush of water became. The Rio Frio frequently flooded during the rainy season and could swell to twice its size and depth. From what he could see in his beam of light, it was well on its way there now. He scanned the area, looking for any kind of opening that might lead to the cavern where Esme had been playing. At first he saw nothing, which was the problem with many of the cave systems in Costa Rica. They were well hidden with foliage, and most had never been mapped. But then he spotted a dark shadow to the side of a moss-covered boulder and knew he'd found the entrance. He trekked through the muddy forest floor to the opening and stuck his head inside, calling, "Esme? Sara? Are you in there?"

Nothing.

Blood thudded in his temples, and his throat dried as he stepped farther inside the mouth of the tunnel. In here, the roar of the rain was silenced, and the flashlight beam bounced off rock walls and the gravel floor. He spotted one of Esme's dolls nearby and his pulse tripped. "Esme? Sara? Where are you?"

Still nothing.

He was about to head back to the others for more flashlights when a small, sharp cry echoed from the shadows of the tunnel.

Esme.

He hiked a bit farther into the tunnel, balancing his weight with a hand on the rock wall to keep from twisting an ankle on the uneven floor. Deeper into the cavern, the slow *drip-drip-drip* of water that was normal inside caves grew into a larger rushing sound as the river outside invaded the underground space. Each time he closed his eyes he pictured Sara wandering down these passages alone, in the dark, searching for the little girl. It was so easy to get disoriented and lost down here, never to be found.

No. He would find her. Even if he had to search forever, he would find Sara.

"Esme? *Dónde estás?*"

Where are you?

"*Hace frío y oscuro y tengo miedo,*" Esme called back, which Gabe took as a good sign. Not that she was cold and in the dark and scared, but that she was well enough to talk to him.

"*¿Estás herido?*" he asked.

Are you hurt?

"*Estoy bien, Tío Gabe, pero Sara está durmiendo y no se despierta.*"

I'm okay, Uncle Gabe, but Sara's sleeping and she won't wake up.

His heart tripped. Sara was with Esme, then. That was good. But she was unconscious or worse. That was bad.

The next question stuck in his throat, but he had to know. "Is Sara breathing, Esme?"

One beat passed, then two. Finally, she said, "*Sí.*"

With each question, Gabe moved closer to

the sound of Esme's voice until he finally reached her—or her location, anyway. A pile of fresh debris covered the tunnel at that point, and water drizzled down from above. His best guess was Esme had come down here to play, Sara had found her, and then the tunnel had partially collapsed from the rain, trapping them.

His relief that Sara was still alive was brief, though, because he soon became aware that that sound of rushing water was growing stronger behind the blockade of rubble in front of him. He suspected that this particular *cavernas* was part of the drainage system for the hills surrounding the village, and if he was right, then all that water trying to reach the river below would just keep building and building until it filled the tunnel and drowned them all.

"Esme? Is there water where you are?" he asked through the tiny cracks between the rocks blocking the tunnel.

"Sí. Está hasta mi cintura."

Yes. It's up to my waist.

His heart tripped. If it was up to the little girl's waist and Sara was unconscious, then her face would be underwater. The words hurt to say, but he had to know. "Where is Sara, Esme? Is she lying on the ground?"

"*Está sentada contra la pared,*" Esme said, and the constriction in Gabe's chest eased.

She's sitting against the wall.

Okay. Okay. Relieved to know that Sara wasn't in imminent danger of drowning just yet, Gabe took a deep breath, his mind whirling with information. He needed to get more light in here so he could see what he was doing. Then he needed to move those damned rocks so he could get them out of there before the water got too high. And he needed the others to be ready for Sara's injuries when they were free.

"Esme?" he called.

"*Sí, Tío Gabe?*" Her little voice caught on a sob. "*Estoy asustada.*"

He closed his eyes and rested his forehead against the cool rocks separating them. "I know, sweetheart. I know. But I'm going to get you out of there. You and Sara both, but I need you to be brave right now, okay? Can you do that for me?"

"*Sí, Tío Gabe.*"

"Good. Now, I need you to make sure you keep your head and Sara's head above water, understand? She's sleeping so she won't know there's water, so you need to take care of her, all right?"

"*Sí.*"

"I need to go back outside to get some things to help me rescue you and—"

"No!" Esme cried. "*¡Por favor! ¡Por favor no me dejes!*"

Please don't leave me.

Once more his mind flashed back to Vukovar, to Marija trapped under debris, bleeding internally, screaming at him to help her, to help Karlo, to not leave them alone again. It broke Gabe's heart, but he knew he had to go, had to get the equipment he needed to clear this debris or he'd never get them out. Time was ticking. There was no alternative.

He gripped the cold, slimy rocks beneath his fingers and said a silent prayer for strength, then said, "I must go. But I swear to you, Esme, I'll be right back. I won't leave you, but I need tools to get you out. Be brave just a little while and sing me a song. Keep singing until I get back so I can find you again, okay? And you need to keep Sara safe, too, while I'm gone, all right?"

A sniffle and a sigh, then, "*¿Qué debo cantar?*"

What should I sing?

He tried to think of a song they both knew. "How about 'Twinkle, Twinkle, Little Star'? Come on, I'll start with you. *Twinkle, twinkle, little star, how I wonder what you are...*"

"Up above the world so high, like a diamond in the sky," Esme continued, and Gabe smiled.

They sang another round together as he set his flashlight up to beam off the ceiling, illuminating the tunnel where he crouched. It was significantly smaller here than at the entrance, with barely room for one adult person, let alone two. Which meant he'd need to work alone to move the debris.

Fine. He'd move mountains on his own if it meant saving Esme and Sara.

"That's it," Gabe said as Esme started through the song for a third time. "Keep singing. Loud as you can so I can hear you. I'm going to get my tools, but I'll be right back. Keep singing!"

He fumbled his way out of the tunnel and back to the entrance. It was still coming down by the bucketful outside and the ground was even more of a muddy mess, but Gabe trudged through it, head down and focus solely on Esme and Sara in that cave.

When he made it back to the house, he

filled the others in on what he knew while he got the crowbar and more flashlights out of the bed of the truck. "They're trapped in a tunnel leading to the cavern. It's some kind of drainage way for the hilltop water. There was a partial collapse, and debris is blocking their exit. Esme is okay. Sara's hurt. I don't know how badly yet, because she's unconscious."

Gabe tried not to think too much about Sara's injuries, because it wouldn't help him get her out at this point. He was distracted enough as it was, and he couldn't afford to lose focus. Not now. Not again.

There was too much at stake.

"I'll come with you," Noah said, moving in beside him as Gabe started back toward the cave, arms laden down with stuff.

"No. It's too narrow inside for more than one person." He looked at the others. "But you can all move closer to the entrance. That way when I do get them out, you'll be right there to help."

A murmur passed through the others as he trekked back toward the cave. It was good they were there. In Vukovar, he'd had no one. Now he had a whole circle of people to help. For so long, he'd tried to lock everything down, keep everyone away. But just then he realized that letting other people in wasn't a burden, it was a blessing.

When he reached the entrance to the tunnel again, the faint sounds of Esme's singing greeted him. He made his way back down the tunnel to where they were, leaving flashlights behind to illuminate their way out. Finally, he was back at the debris, and he got to work with the crowbar, feeling like he was finally making progress.

"Esme?" he said, when the singing stopped. "What's going on over there?"

"Cold," she said, teeth chattering. "Very cold."

Hypothermia. Not good.

"Where is the water now?" he asked, poking and digging at the wall of debris and managing to knock a few smaller rocks aside, only to have water start trickling through. Oh, boy. His pulse tripled. "Esme? How's Sara?"

"Still sleeping," she said. "I'm sleepy, too."

"No!" Gabe yelled, his voice booming off the rock walls. "No, Esme! You must stay awake. Do you hear me? Do not go to sleep. You stay awake and you sing to me, okay?"

"Twinkle, twinkle, little star," her tiny voice sang again, weaker this time.

Damn.

Gabe's digging grew more desperate. If Esme fell asleep and they both went under, they'd drown.

Can't lose them. Won't lose them.

More rocks fell, enough that he could see into the shadows on the other side. Esme, small and shaking as she leaned against the rock wall, her lips bluish and her complexion gray with exhaustion and cold. Sara beside her, her head resting on Esme's shoulder. The water had risen up to their chests now and was gushing through the debris wall in spurts, clouding his vision and nearly washing away his crowbar before he caught it.

"Keep singing, Esme. Keep singing. I've almost got you out." He reached through the opening and shook her little shoulder when she closed her eyes and went silent. "Esme, stay with me. You must stay with me! Do not go to sleep!"

"But I'm so tired, Uncle Gabe," she whined, squinting at him. "Want a nap."

"You can nap when we get out of here, okay? You can take a nice long nap with your daddy at home in your own bed, okay? You want to see your daddy again, yes?"

"*Sí...*" Esme mumbled.

Beside her, Sara moaned, and her eyelids

fluttered but didn't open. She had a grayish pallor, too, her lips blue as well, and there appeared to be a fairly nasty gash near her right temple.

His pulse stuttered. She was still alive. There was still a chance.

"Okay. Good. Keep singing, sweetheart. We're almost out."

More water gushed out from between the rocks and the flashlight behind him skittered away down the tunnel toward the entrance, but Gabe didn't care. It was dark. It was dank. It was dangerous as hell. And he refused to stop until they were all safe and sound.

Esme's singing died off, and silence pressed in around him, suffocating.

"Esme?" Gabe called. "Esme, talk to me."

No response.

He hauled off and struck the wall of debris with every ounce of strength he had, and between that and the pressure of the water on the other side, the whole thing burst free. He was tumbled backward as the entire tunnel gave way and burst open, tossing them all out into the raging river. Gabe shook the water out of his face and scanned the area, but there was no sign of Esme or Sara.

"Help!" he yelled, then dived underwater to

look for them. It was lighter outside now, but between the strong currents and the rain, the water was too cloudy to see much. He broke the surface again and screamed, "Help me!"

He went under and held his breath, searching and searching until his lungs burned before resurfacing again. Still nothing.

"Help me! Help me, please!" he bellowed over and over until his voice grew hoarse, diving under then resurfacing again, praying to God that someone would hear him, that someone would come to help.

Marija's face flashed in his head like lightning. She was holding Karlo and they were both smiling. Their injuries were gone and they looked happy and healthy, like they were waiting for him to join them. Gabe fought the currents, but it was a losing battle. Water raged around him, and he was cold, so cold. His eyes felt heavy and he was tired, too tired. It would be so easy to give up, to just let go, to stop fighting…

"Gabe!" a voice yelled from the forest, followed by a bright beam of light blinding him.

He squinted and held up a hand to see Noah and Carlos and Matteo and Doreen, all hurrying down the muddy riverbank. Help was here. Help had arrived this time. He wasn't alone. His fight wasn't over. He spat out a mouthful of river water and shouted as best he could. "Sara and Esme are in here. We need to find them!"

Noah dived in immediately, searching the area along with Gabe. A few second later, he resurfaced with Esme in his arms. "I've got the little one!"

That left Sara. Gabe dived again. And again. Each time coming up empty.

Muscles shaking and pulse thundering, he took another deep breath and prepared to go under once more. Then something brushed his leg and he took a chance, ducking his head into the raging water and grasping a wrist. Sara! He pulled them both to the surface, then swam as hard as he could for shore, holding her above water with one arm while paddling with the other.

What felt like an eternity later, he reached land and pulled Sara onto the shore. Checked her pulse and felt none. Dammit. Started CPR, chest compressions then breaths, chest compression then breaths.

More memories returned. Doing CPR on Karlo for hours, waiting and waiting for help to arrive. Help that never came. Watching as he lost Marija as well, his bad decision costing them all.

Then, from behind him a cough, small but strong.

"She's back. She's okay," Noah said. "Esme's okay."

"Come on," Gabe whispered to Sara. "Don't leave me. Don't you dare leave me. I need you, Sara. I love you, Sara."

He bent to give her more breaths, and her eyelids fluttered. Gabe straightened slightly. "Sara? *Dušo?*"

She moaned again, then rolled slightly as she coughed up water. He held her, never so glad in his life to be thrown up on. Finally, she lay on her back again and frowned up at him. "What happened? Why does my head hurt?"

"You were trapped in the tunnel, probably knocked on the head by debris. I think you may have a concussion." He cupped her cheek, smiling down at her, blinking back tears. She was safe. She was okay. She hadn't left him. Maybe, if he was lucky, she never would. Without thinking, without reservation, he said, "I love you, Sara."

For a moment, she just blinked up at him. Then she clasped his wrist and smiled back at him. "I love you, too, Gabe. And I'm sorry about our fight last night. I should never have said what I did."

"And I should never had gone to that bar," he said, kissing her hand. "Or kept that phone number. I swear, that woman means nothing to me. Only you. Always you, *dušo*."

Sara laughed, then winced, tentatively touching her injured temple. "This is going to be complicated."

Gabe grinned, rain dripping off his face, mud all around them, yet it felt like paradise. "The best things always are."

CHAPTER SIXTEEN

Sara woke up in the ward tent the next morning, her head pounding and her heart light. It was still hard to believe what had happened the night before—the cave rescue, Gabe's confession of love.

He loves me.

And I love him.

She squinted up at the bright white ceiling of the tent and let the sounds of the ward wash around her for a while. Monitors beeping, the low murmur of conversations, a small voice singing "Twinkle, Twinkle, Little Star."

Esme.

Slowly, to avoid making the dizziness worse, Sara propped herself up on one elbow and peered over at the bed across from hers. The little girl sat on her bed playing with her doll, a bandage wrapped around one arm.

"Hey," Sara croaked. Her throat felt like

dry as a desert, which was funny, since she'd almost drowned the night before. "How are you, Esme?"

The little girl looked up at Sara, then climbed off her bed and walked over, looking a bit sheepish. "I'm sorry I got you hurt in the cave."

"Aw." She reached over and brushed back the dark hair from the girl's forehead. Even with a concussion, she understood Spanish much better now. Gabe had been right about that. About a lot of things, actually. "It's okay. I'm just glad you're all right."

"Daddy says I owe you a debt of attitude," Esme said, struggling with her English.

Sara bit back a smile. "Gratitude. And you tell him it was no problem at all."

"What was no problem?" Gabe asked, poking his head around the corner of the divider separating Sara's section from the others in the ward.

"*Tío Gabe!*" Esme ran over and wrapped an arm around his scrub-covered legs and held on tight.

"*Buenos días*, Esme," he said, reaching down and swooping her up in his arms. "*Cómo está hoy?*"

"*Mucho mejor, gracias.*" She giggled and hid her face in Gabe's shoulder.

Sara laughed then lay back down on her pillow. "I do believe you'll have a fan for life right there."

"Hmm." He put Esme back on her bed, whispered something to her and kissed her head, then came over to Sara's bedside. "And how are you feeling this morning, *dušo*?"

While he fiddled with the bandages on her head and examined her wound, Sara sighed and did her best to relax. It was always different, being on this side of things, and the adage wasn't wrong—usually medical people did make the worst patients, probably because they kept trying to self-diagnose.

"Any dizziness? Nausea? Blurred vision? Headaches?" Gabe asked, scowling at her chart now, not looking at her, in full doctor mode.

"Yes, no, no, yes." She clasped her hands atop her chest and blinked up at him. "Considering what I went through last night, I feel remarkably good today. How about you, Sir Galahad?"

"Sir what?" He scrunched his nose and glanced her way at last. "I'm fine."

"Come here." She waggled her fingers at him.

He made a few notations on her file, then set it aside, pulling the curtain the rest of the way around her bed for more privacy. He sat on the edge of her cot and took her hand. "What?"

"Thank you for saving me." She squeezed his fingers. "I know that couldn't have been easy for you, after what happened to your family back in Croatia. And I want you to know I appreciate it."

Gabe kissed her fingers then grinned. "You're welcome, *dušo*. I will accept kisses as payment."

"I'm serious."

"As am I." He leaned down and brushed his lips across hers, so gently it felt like a feather. "And yes, it was difficult for me. But also freeing. Saving you and Esme last night felt like I'd finally repaid a debt I'd owed in full." He took a deep breath and stared at their entwined fingers. "Perhaps it's wrong of me to think that way, but I finally feel free."

"I don't think it's wrong at all." Sara reached up with her free hand to cup his cheek. "And I still mean what I said last night. I love you."

"I love you, too."

"Good. Now what are we going to do about it?"

He frowned. "Well, I know what I'd like

to do about it, but this really isn't the place for it, so…"

"I'm not talking about that." She smacked his arm playfully. "And stop avoiding the subject. No more walls between us, okay?"

"Okay." Gabe sighed. "I was up late last night thinking about this, actually."

"And?"

"And I think I'm done here."

Now it was her turn to scowl. "At Hospital Los Cabreras? But you love it here."

"I do. But I love you more, *dušo*." He held up a hand to stop her protest. "But the truth is, I've been hiding out here for a long time. Avoiding life. Avoiding everything to not get hurt again."

"Oh, Gabe."

"That's not really living, though. You made me see that. By coming here, all on your own, taking chances, braving the unknown—"

"Well, I don't know how brave it was, exactly…"

"Stop, *dušo*. Please. You're the bravest woman I know. Striking out on your own, going after what's right for you, for what you deserve, not settling for what's safe. You risked everything coming here, just for an adventure. You risked your life last night to save Esme."

She winced. "Yeah. I'm sorry about that, too. It was reckless of me to charge off like that without knowing what I was doing." Sara exhaled slow. "That was my control issues front and center again. You made me see what a mistake those are. How I need to trust people more. How I need to trust you more, Gabe. You're the best, most honorable and courageous man I know."

He kissed her again, a bit longer and deeper this time. When he sat back, they were both a little breathless.

"So…" he said. "What now?"

"So, I think we need to talk about how we're going to handle this after clinic is over next week. I'm due back at the hospital at the beginning of June. That's when my sabbatical is over."

"Okay." He nodded. "Then I'll talk to Tristan."

"About what?"

"About finding a replacement for me here."

"Wait." Her brows knit as she eased up onto her elbows. "What?"

"Sara, I'm done hiding here. I love this place—you're right. And I will always have fond memories and ties here, but I'm ready to live again. With you, if you'll have me."

A slow smile spread across her face. "Of course I'll have you. But what will you do for work?"

"Well—" He leaned across her legs, resting his elbow on the cot on the other side of her, looking relaxed and handsome as hell. Her heart leaped with the knowledge that he was hers and would be for a very long time, if she had anything to say about it. "One of the things I did last night because I couldn't sleep was get on the internet and check out the hospitals in Chicago. Turns out several of them have openings in their emergency departments."

Her pulse sped up a bit. "Yeah?"

"Yes." He grinned up at her. "So, I put my résumé in for a couple of them, and we'll see where they go. I'd need a place to live there, of course. And—"

"You can live with me," she blurted out, then stopped, cheeks hot. "I mean, I've got plenty of room, now that Luke's moved out and it's just me and the dog there now, so…"

"You have a dog?"

"Yep. A lab named Boomer. You'll love him. Everyone does."

"I'm sure I will," Gabe said, leaning in to steal another kiss. "I already love his owner."

"Does this mean we're officially a couple then?" Sara asked between kisses. "Because I'm totally okay with that."

"I believe it does, Nurse Parker." Gabe nuzzled her neck. "It certainly does."

CHAPTER SEVENTEEN

One year later

SARA CLOSED HER EYES, the salt from the Pacific Ocean filling her lungs. From the front, the Costa Rican resort where they were spending their honeymoon was just a simple three-story white rectangle with a dash of palm trees lining the lawn. But beyond the building, there was nothing but blue-green waves as far as the eye could see. Paradise indeed.

"You sure you don't want to stay longer?" Sara asked her son, Luke, who'd flown in with his girlfriend for the wedding ceremony a few days prior. With his honey-brown hair and ridiculously long lashes, he looked far too much like his father for her comfort. But she loved him more than life itself. "Gabe and I would love to have you guys around. We could catch up some more, spend more time with Michelle. Things seem like they're getting pretty serious between you two."

"Mom, stop." Luke chuckled, his cheeks pink. "And yeah, I'm sure. I'd love to stay, but we have to get home for finals next week. She's got a lot of studying to do for her MCATs, and I've got a big project due for my architectural final."

"Okay, okay." She smoothed down the collar of his polo shirt, then tried to tidy his hair before he pushed her hands away. Once a mother, always a mother. "Well, be careful and travel safe. Call me when you get back to the States."

"Will do." He kissed her cheek, then took off, his wheeled suitcase clacking on the tile floor of the hotel. He and his girlfriend locked arms and disappeared around the corner.

"Such a nice kid," Doreen said from behind her. Sara turned to find her friend and Matteo, his arms around Doreen from behind. They made a handsome couple, too, and she was so happy Doreen had found another soul mate after losing her Martin. "Too bad they're leaving so soon."

"Yeah, they had to get back." She leaned her elbows on the railing and stared out at the ocean again. Before, she would've been filled with worries, obsessing over what she could do to try and control the situation, but now she let it go. That was all thanks to Gabe. He'd taught her how to trust again—other people and herself. Just one of the many gifts he'd given her. She glanced at Matteo, then did a double take. "Where's your mustache?"

"Shaved it off." He ran a hand over his now clean-shaven upper lip. Without it, he looked ten years younger. "Needed a change, and Doreen didn't really care for it."

"Hey, don't blame it on me. It's your face, honey. Do what you want with it." She winked at Sara. "Even if you want to cover it up with that monstrosity."

Sara laughed, then pulled them each into a tight hug. "I wish you guys didn't have to go, too. I'm going to miss you both. It was great seeing you again."

"Same here." Doreen pulled back, blinking hard against the tears sparkling in her eyes. She looked much younger and happier, too, since she'd moved down here permanently to be with Matteo. They split their time between San José, where he had his dental practice, and Hospital Los Cabreras, where they both still volunteered. "But we'll see you both in December again when you come back to work with the charity, right?"

"Right." Sara sniffled and smiled through her tears. "I don't even know why I'm crying so much."

"Happy tears?" Doreen hugged her again, then stepped back to take Matteo's hand. "You've got my new cell number, yes?"

"Happy tears." She waved as they left. "And yes."

They disappeared into the enormous lobby crowded with guests, and Sara turned to head back up to the room where Gabe waited. He'd already said his goodbyes earlier at breakfast, and she knew that was the hardest part for him. He had the door open for her before she even knocked, and she slipped in under his arm.

The resort wasn't as ornate or elaborate as some she'd seen, but there was air-conditioning. Sweet, precious air-conditioning. And with the sweltering rain forest heat in full force these days, that alone made it seem like the most luxurious place she'd ever stayed.

"Man, that feels incredible." Noah's voice echoed down the hall, and he lifted his arms and spun around before waving in their direction. He and Tristan had booked the suite next to theirs for the week. "What are you lovebirds up to? Want to join us at the pool?"

"No, thanks," Gabe said, looping an arm around Sara's waist in the doorway. He still had a thing about water from the whole river incident, Sara knew, though he'd never admit it to anyone.

"I'll come down later," she said, then waited until Noah and Tristan were gone before facing Gabe. "So, whatever will we do to fill our day?"

"I have a few ideas." He raised a dark brow at her and pulled her closer. She couldn't have protested if she wanted. Not with his hands on her hips and his warmth pressed against her. Sara raised on tiptoe and kissed him. The way he smiled when she pulled away lit her insides on fire.

"Sounds perfect to me." Sara grinned.

Before they went back inside, she took one last look out the windows at either end of the hall. On one side was the lush green of the rain forest. On the other was the bright blue of the ocean. Just like their life now. They both lived and worked in Chicago—Sara back in her PICU, Gabe in the ER at Chicago Memorial—for most of the year, but they returned to their beloved rain forest, the place where they'd met, the place where they'd fallen in love, whenever they could.

Sara stopped moving and stared out at the courtyard, not really seeing it. Seemed everything was changing without her. Or with her. She'd never been big on change, always rushing to anticipate things before they happened to avoid disaster. With Luke. With her patients. With everything. Hard to believe that just a year ago, she'd never been here, never known Gabe, never met Doreen and Matteo and all the other good friends she'd made here.

Her sabbatical, and her life, had turned out much different than she'd expected, but so much better than Sara ever could've imagined.

Then Gabe picked her up, and she forgot about everything except him and the wonderful love they shared. She wrapped her legs around his waist as he kicked the door closed behind them, then pinned her against the heavy door, Sara shivered as he slid his hands up the outsides of her thighs, taking her pink cotton sundress with them. His tongue dueled with hers, and she squirmed to get the dress over her head and kicked her flip-flops off, leaving her naked except for her underwear.

"You have too many clothes on, husband," she said against his lips as he carried her to bed, stumbling over their bags but keeping his mouth pressed to hers. Gabe laid her down and took a step back, swallowing hard as his gaze swept over her body, and Sara blushed under his stare. They might be married, but he was still the only man who'd ever looked at her like that, like she was some Greek statue come to life, like she was perfect.

Then he pulled off his shirt and crawled onto the bed beside her, and nope. He was the perfect one. All toned and taut and all hers. Their lips met in another sizzling kiss, and he tasted of wine from the minibar and wicked need. His bare chest rubbed hers, teasing her sensitive nipples, and she moaned into his mouth, a wildfire roaring inside her, working its way to her core. She ran her hands down his stomach, and his muscles tensed beneath her touch. Smiling, Sara dipped her fingers below the waistband of his shorts, enjoying the low rumble of his groans, then slid her hands back up to his shoulders before sinking her fingers into his dark hair. He was hard against her—so hard, so hot—and she arched her hips, desperate for friction.

He circled her waist and lifted, pulling off her panties, then tugging her to the edge of the mattress so her legs dangled over his shoulders. He bent low to trace his tongue over her slick folds. She loved it when he took charge in bed like this and couldn't contain her gasp, tilting her hips as he made love to her with his mouth and fingers.

Desire made her limbs heavy as Gabe spread her legs wider. She closed her eyes, her head falling back on the bed. His warm breath between her thighs was both unbearable and everything all at once. He looked up at her, and their eyes met, and even in the shadows, his eyes burned with desire. She slid her hands into his hair, pulling him closer, riding the waves of pleasure all the way to the peak of ecstasy.

"You're beautiful," he murmured, cupping her breasts.

"No, you are." She buried her face into his neck and guided him inside her.

"Sara. My Sara." He looked up at her from beneath heavy eyelids as she rode him slow and steady. Then he took charge, guiding her movements, building the friction between until they were both on the brink of climax. Gabe shifted his weight, rolling her beneath him, thrusting hard once, twice, as he reached between them to stroke her most sensitive flesh, until they both came hard.

A long time later, after they'd floated back down to earth, she whispered, "I love you."

"I love you, too, wife. Now and forever."

"Now and forever," Sara whispered back before they both drifted off into blissful sleep.

* * * * *

If you enjoyed this story, check out these other great reads from Traci Douglass

Her One-Night Secret
The Vet's Unexpected Hero
Neurosurgeon's Christmas to Remember
Their Hot Hawaiian Fling

All available now!